CHRISTMAS THEN

Ten Stories

Charles Robert Baker

This book is a work of fiction. Names, characters, businesses, organizations, places, and events are either a product of the author's imagination or are used fictitiously.

CHRISTMAS THEN: TEN STORIES

Printed in the United States of America. No part of this book may be used or reproduced in any manner without the express written consent of the author except in the case of brief excerpts embedded in articles or critical reviews.

ISBN: 9781977850843

First edition: October 2019

DEDICATION

For Candace and Charlotte;
without whom.....well, I don't even want to think about that.

THE STORIES

ACKNOWLEDGMENTS

The author would like to thank the late Mae Godwin Matkin and Charles Robert Matkin for taking care of him when he was little and encouraging his curiosity and imagination. There is not a day goes by when he does not think of you; he lost you both much too early.

WHAT MISS JOHNSON TAUGHT

In the summer of 1956, on the day after the last day of school, Thomas Godwin was sent to live with his mother's folks in Dallas. His mom and dad were "working through a difficult time" and this chance to get away from all that suited him just fine. He loved the big house where voices were low and respectful and doors were opened and closed gently and summer days rolled along peacefully predictable. There was a good fishing lake to the east and a small shopping center with the best model kit hobby shop he had ever seen to the west and both were an easy walk for a seven-year-old boy. He made a couple of friends, in that quick way boys can, and after breakfast, after his grandfather had left for the Cotton Exchange, Thomas would hug his grandmother goodbye, grab his tackle box and pole and take off up the alley to find Jon and they would get Teddy. Together they would laugh and shove and trip their way to the pier for a morning of serious fishing. Rainy days they would gather in one or the other's den and play board games such as Waterloo and Gettysburg. Then there were those days Thomas chose to stay in his room working on a model ship and reading from his treasured collection of "Classics Illustrated." These were the days he missed his mother terribly but as much as he missed her, he hoped he would not have to return to Amarillo and that loud life they lived with his father. His grandparents called his mother often and sometimes through his door he could hear his grandfather's voice rise then his grandmother's but they would quickly hush and after a quiet while one of them would come to his room and say,

"Your mama wants to say goodnight to you.".

He would get on the phone and exchange "I miss you"s and "I love you"s but his mother never mentioned what was going on or what would happen next and he never asked. Thomas held tightly to the belief that if he didn't bring up the fact that school was about to start and he should be going back to Amarillo maybe no one else would either and this summer life would simply go on.

᷿

One Saturday morning, during an unusually quite breakfast, his grandfather suddenly cleared his throat and said,

"Thomas!"

Well, this startled the boy so badly that his half-swallowed orange juice sprayed out over his half-finished breakfast plate. Allowing a few moments for his wife to clear the mess and for Thomas to pull himself together, his grandfather continued,

"This is the weekend you would normally be returning to Amarillo but your mother and grandmother and I have come to the conclusion that it would be best if you stayed on here. What do you think about that?"

This last was accompanied by a sharp slap on the back and Thomas held his breath trying to control a powerful attack of the hiccups.

"Well, speak up, speak up! Cat got your tongue?"

His grandfather was clearly enjoying this.

"Goodness, Carl, give the boy a minute or two to let this sink in. There now Thomas, you just relax, take some deep breaths. Here let me wipe this juice off your chin."

The hiccups were not to be controlled and Thomas did not know whether to laugh or cry, so he did both.

Thomas' life took a new turn and his days filled up quickly and he was happier than he could ever remember being. The uncomfortable newness of Lakewood Elementary was made bearable by the fact that Jon and Teddy were in most of his classes. New clothes, new school supplies, new teachers; every aspect of his life was new, and Thomas was cautiously joyful. Perhaps the strangest new addition was church; Thomas had never been in one and that fact had long been a source of argument between his grandparents and his parents. Now that they had been granted temporary custody, the Matkins could introduce their grandson to the congregation they had been members of for a very long time. So, one Sunday morning near the end of September, Thomas, in his new suit, complete with a clip-on bow tie, found himself seated in a chilly little room on the second floor of the cathedral's education building following along with the other children the lesson being taught by the third-grade Sunday School teacher, Miss Johnson. Thomas took to her at once; he guessed she was about as old as his grandmother, tall and thin with a sweet, soft voice. She had written her name on the blackboard, and Thomas thought it was the strangest name he had ever heard of: Siddie Joe Johnson. But wait, he knew that name! Where had he seen it before? He couldn't remember.

Sunday school consisted of a class period, followed by a children's chapel service, then all the students were herded across the parking lot and into the massive cathedral where they sat in the back until the grownups service was ended. Thomas was in awe of everything about the grand, old, Gothic cathedral; the way the light through the stained glass moved across the congregation during the service, the music, the liturgy, the vestments. All of it.

After the service, the congregation filed out through the front doors where the dean met with each member. Thomas' grandparents were very proud to introduce their grandson and the dean gave the boy a firm handshake and said he hoped he would see him again next Sunday. After looking up at his grandfather, who gave him a wink and a nod, Thomas was happy to tell the dean,

"Yes sir, I'll be here all right!"

There were refreshments in the Great Hall and several people approached the Matkins to meet this new little boy; one of them was his teacher, Miss Johnson.

"So, Clara and Carl, this is the young lad I have heard so much about."

"Yes, this is our Thomas," said Clara.

"Well, I must tell you I am very impressed with his reading skills; they are far in advance of most his age. He breezed through this morning's lesson with no problems at all."

"Oh, Thomas is a whiz when it comes to reading," Carl boasted.

"What do you like to read most, Thomas," Miss Johnson asked.

"Just about everything, Miss Johnson, but I like stories best."

"Ah, a fiction lover! Good," said Miss Johnson. "Did you know we have a children's library here, Thomas?"

"No ma'am."

"Then let me show it to you. Clara, you and Carl stay here and enjoy your coffee and we will be right back."

Miss Johnson took Thomas by the hand and led him down a long hallway in the education building. There at the end was a room of neatly arranged books on shelves that were just the right height for children.

"Miss Wren," said Miss Johnson, "I have a new reader for you. Meet Thomas Godwin, Clara and Carl's grandson."

"I am very pleased to meet you, Master Godwin. Come with me to the desk and I will fill out a borrower's card for you. You are allowed two books at a time and you may keep them for two weeks."

Miss Wren finished filling out a card and put it in a little wooden file box.

"There, you are now an official borrower! Congratulations!"

"May I borrow a book today?" Thomas asked.

"Yes, of course. Pick any two you like and have them back here in two weeks."

Thomas browsed the shelves while Miss Johnson and Miss Wren discussed whatever it is that grownups discuss when they are not talking to children. Thomas read the labels on the bookshelves: Biography, Science, History, Fiction, Poetry...He recognized a title in the History section, Texas: The Land of the Tejas, that was one of his textbooks at school. Then the light went on in his head. He pulled the book from the shelf, looked at the name on the cover and ran to where the two ladies were talking.

"Miss Johnson!" he shouted, "this is your book!"

It came out sounding more like a question than a declaration and Miss Johnson laughed and said, "Yes, I'm proud to say it is."

"You mean you wrote all the words and everything?"

The boy was clearly amazed.

"Oh, Miss Johnson has written many books, young Thomas," said Miss Wren. "Here let me show you."

"Now Dolly, let the boy explore on his own."

"Siddie Joe, you know better than most that it is a librarian's duty to guide the explorers. Here, Master Godwin, this is one you will surely like, Cat Hotel. And how about a book of poetry? This is Feather in My Hand. Do you like to read poems?"

Thomas admitted that he couldn't remember if he had ever read a poem on his own before, but added that his mother liked poetry a lot and would read poems to him at bedtime. It was a sad remembrance and the two ladies saw that it was.

"It's time I took you back to your grandparents, Thomas. Thank you, Dolly, I'll see you at lunch."

"Thank you, Miss Wren," said Thomas.

"Enjoy your books, dear boy, and come back in two weeks and tell me how you liked them."

In the back seat of the car as the Matkins drove home, Thomas opened the poetry book and read:

"I live in a country of gulls—

Land and water and birds.

This is too lovely a thing

Ever to put into words."

He wanted more than anything to read this to his mother.

On Saturday mornings Thomas was given an allowance, something he had never heard of before. But he had to earn it; he was responsible for keeping his room and bathroom clean, keep his grades up, help grandmother set the table for meals, and, his favorite, clean the ashes out of the fireplace and lay on logs for the evening fire; his grandfather expected a cozy fire to be waiting for him when he came home from the office. Money in his pocket, Thomas would take off after breakfast to Hillside Village for a new model at JoJo's Toys or some comic books and a soda at John Cobb's Drug Store. His days and his mind were filled as full as they could be but there was an empty place in his heart and this nagged at him something awful during quiet, still times. One Saturday afternoon, after he had lit a fire in the den, and he and his grandfather had settled in to watch some Westerns, he could stand it no longer.

"Grandfather, I gotta know what's going on."

"What's going on with what, Thomas?"

"You know. What's going on with my mom and dad?"

His grandfather looked at him for a long time and finally said, "All right, here it is. You remember how hard things were between them before you came down for the summer?"

"I sure do."

"Of course you do. You were right in the middle of it. Well, things have been getting worse and now it seems your daddy has taken off and according to him, he won't be coming back this time."

"You talked to him?"

"I sure did. He called from Shreveport wanting money."

"Did you send him any?"

"No sir, I did not!"

"What did you say to him?" Thomas could not imagine anyone not obeying his father.

"I'd rather not say, but understand this – he is gone for good. I suspect that is more of a relief than a sadness to you. Am I right?"

"I guess so. Did he ask about me?"

"No sir, he did not."

His grandmother brought in a bowl of sliced apples that she had sprinkled with salt. Thomas helped himself and asked, "What's mom doing?"

"Not too very darn much!", his grandfather shouted, throwing an apple slice into the fire.

"Carl," his grandmother said, "let me. Thomas, your mother just seems to be kind of stuck. We've offered to come get her and bring her home but she says she feels frozen in place and can't think what to do."

"Seems to me," Thomas said, "that leaving something bad to go to something good wouldn't require much thinking. Why won't she do it?"

"We don't know, Thomas."

~

The next morning in Sunday school, Miss Johnson began her lesson. "Children, this Sunday is the fourth Sunday in Advent. Christmas is just days away. Next Sunday in fact! Isn't it exciting? I'm sure we are looking forward to Santa and presents, aren't we? I know I am! But let's take this morning to remember how all this started. Do you remember? Remember Mary and the Angel Gabriel? Sure you do. You remember how Gabriel had an announcement to make – an Annunciation? He announced to Mary that she had been chosen by God for something very special. How did this make Mary feel? Remember, she was afraid. What was she afraid of? The Gospels don't help us much there, but let's try to imagine. There she was, a young lady with no husband, and she was told she will have a son. And the story of how this would happen! Who would believe it? Her parents? Her friends? Her boyfriend, Joseph? Probably not. You think they would look down their nose at her and talk about her behind her back and make her feel bad and guilty and ashamed? Probably so. I think all this must have run through Mary's mind and scared her. But Mary was smart. She knew that the only thing she would have to be ashamed of was choosing not to do what she knew in her heart was right."

It hit Thomas like a snowball to the back of the head! "That's it!", he thought, "that's what's wrong with mom! She's scared of what people will think because dad left her!"

He scribbled Miss Johnson's words down on his worksheet. When he got home, he pulled out a piece of red construction paper and a green marker from his desk drawer. He wrote, "The only thing to be ashamed of is not doing what you know in your heart to be right" in the center of the page. He glued on a cutout of a Christmas tree, a wreath and a candy cane, then folded it carefully, slipped it into an envelope, addressed it, found a stamp in his grandfather's desk and ran to the mailbox at the corner. "This should do the trick," he said, and slid it through the slot.

ಾ

The last days before Christmas go by so slowly for a child. Even with all the decorating, baking, shopping, wrapping and all the other activities. And on top of everything else, Thomas had been asked to serve as an acolyte at the Christmas Eve Family Service; even so, Thomas felt like each day had been extended to forty-eight hours. There had been no word from his mother. The last time his grandfather had tried to reach her by phone, the operator told him the number was no longer in service. Thomas moped through these joyous, festive days and his grandparents understood that there was only one person who could lift this weight from his heart. By Christmas Eve, he gave up hoping. Late afternoon, Thomas and Jon and the others met in the basement of the cathedral, slipped into their vestments, and went through one more rehearsal. The priest in charge of the children was a very nervous young man who wanted everything to go perfectly; this made everyone anxious and it took a long time before Thomas got his part right. He wanted desperately to be excused but he remembered Miss Johnson's words, the ones he had sent his mother, so when the organ sounded and voices raised in song, he had no choice but to follow through. The grand procession ended at the altar and now, as the service went on and on and on, Thomas knelt in his place in the acolyte's pew, his hands folded in prayer on the rail that divided him from the people filing by on their way to the high altar. The air was close. The powerful aromas from the bee's wax candles and the strong incense and the overheated air made Thomas feel faint. He rested his head on his forearms and prayed that this would all be over soon. Then there was a hand on his. He looked up and there she was, standing in line to receive the mystery. People went around her as she just stood there smiling a smile that was every bit as bright as that star of long ago and far away. Before Thomas's eyes were completely awash with tears, he saw a piece of red construction paper sticking out of her coat pocket.

THE CAT IN THE CREEK

Coffee was young Thomas's alarm clock; by the time the scent had wafted down the hallway of the big house on East Mockingbird Lane and reached his nose, he knew it was time to get up. It was a cold, bright December morning in 1957; the fear and anxiety that had been caused by the tornado that whipped through the Oak Cliff and Love Field areas last April were replaced by another possible menace in October: the Russian satellite, Sputnik. But these were grown-up worries; Thomas was more interested in the adventures of a boy in a new TV show, a boy his own age named Beaver.

The floor was cold and Thomas put on his slippers and robe and sat down with his grandfather in the breakfast room. It was still odd for Thomas to see the dapper gentleman dressed in khakis on a weekday morning. Normally, Carl Matkin would be wearing his usual monogrammed white dress shirt, striped tie, black suit pants held up by suspenders, monogrammed cuff links and tie bar but, since he decided to take the month of December off, figuring the Cotton Exchange could get along fine without him for a few weeks, his wardrobe had changed dramatically. That was not all that had changed. His wife, Clara, thought she would go stark raving mad having Carl around the house all day trying to be helpful. He was a restless pest who followed her from room to room. She loved the man dearly but too much of him was too much! The day came when she had had enough.

"Carl, get in the car right now and drive yourself to Adam's Hobby Shop! Pick a hobby, any hobby that will fill your time! You are driving me crazy!"

The shock on the old man's face touched Clara's heart; she kissed his rough cheek (he had, to her horror, decided to grow a beard!) and said,

"It's for the good of both of us, dear. I am trying to keep you alive and myself out of prison."

The result of this was Carl's discovery that he had an amazing, previously unknown, talent for woodworking. He started with little things: bookends, a magazine rack, a bookcase for Thomas's room; and as his belief in his own talent grew, so did the number of tools. With the help of his good friend, Captain Forrester of the fire department, half of the Matkin's garage was soon a fully equipped workshop. Carl was a happy man, and visions of retirement danced in his head like sugarplums.

"Good morning, Thomas! Well, here it is; the last school day before your long Christmas vacation. Are you excited?"

"I sure am, Grandfather. We have a party today, and the big kids sing in the auditorium and we get turkey and dressing in the cafeteria! And then we get to go to the film room and watch A Christmas Carol."

"Well, I know you'll enjoy that. You must have read the Classics Illustrated version a hundred times!"

"Yes sir, and before I could read it myself, you used to read it to me."

Grandmother came in with Thomas's breakfast, a hot plate of bacon and eggs. Oh, more wonderful aromas to blend with the coffee and the toast that had just jumped from the toaster!

"Eat up, honey," she said. "Your mother has already had hers and she needs to leave for the school just as soon as you are ready."

"Okay, Grandmother."

In a flash, Thomas was dressed and ready to go. He had Christmas cards to give to his classmates and a platter of Christmas cookies for the party. But before getting in the car, he had to pass his mother's final inspection.

"Teeth brushed? Hands washed? Let me see your fingernails. Good job. There is just one thing…"

Thomas knew what it was; he could never manage to get a straight part in his thick brown hair. Mae corrected that and declared her son suitable to be shown to the world and they were off. Carl waved good-bye to them as Mae backed out of the driveway, then closed himself in his workshop to put the finishing touches on his Christmas project: a large stable and manger to display in the front yard. Back in October, with the help of the cathedral secretary, he had ordered plastic figures from a catalog of all the people and animals that had gathered on that night so long ago and so far away. There they all were, crowded uncomfortably together in a corner of the garage and Carl was sure that when everything was put in place and lit up, cars on East Mockingbird Lane would slow down to admire his work.

☙

The school festivities were great fun. Thomas and his best friend Jon Forrester laughed and sang and ate and Jon asked the teacher if he could tell a joke to the class. "Go ahead, Jon, if you feel you must," said the amazingly patient Miss Woolf, who had endured

Jon's non-stop comic act for nearly four months with grace and poise. "Okay, here goes," announced Jon. "Why does a shark swim in saltwater? Give up? Because swimming in pepper water makes him sneeze!" The class exploded with laughter, no one laughing longer or louder than Jon himself. Mrs. Woolf merely groaned and looked at the wall clock where she was relieved to see that it was nearly time to end the school day and begin the holiday break.

"That was quick! Why don't regular school days go by that fast?" Jon asked, as the two walked across the schoolyard towards their homes.

Thomas answered, "Because they're not as fun as today. Fun always goes fast."

"Well, it seems like a big gyp to me," Jon declared.

The sunny day had turned dark; the grey clouds looked heavy and they hung low to the ground. And the air was much colder that it had been in the morning.

"I bet it snows!" Jon said.

"Wouldn't that be great? I hope it snows all the way to Christmas Day!" Thomas said. The friends parted at the corner of Jon's street with promises to see each other on Christmas Eve. Jon had family in town from Corpus Christi and he was going to be stuck for several days entertaining some cousin he hardly knew. He declared that to be a "big gyp" too. Several times!

The wind was picking up and Thomas felt the cold even through all the layers of clothes he was wearing. He decided to run the rest of the way home and had gone just about a block when he saw the biggest boy in school directly ahead of him: Big Freddy Slack! Big Freddy was a sixth-grader but he had been held back a couple of years so he was near to being fourteen! All the kids were afraid of him; some of the teachers, too! Big Freddy saw Thomas and yelled, "Where ya runnin' to Tommy? Hurryin' to see Santy Claus?"

Big Freddy let loose one of his evil laughs and Thomas (who hated being called "Tommy") changed direction and ran even faster.

"Don't you run away from me when I'm talkin' to you, you little runt! Come back here!"

"Does he really think I'm stupid enough to do that?" Thomas wondered as he picked up his pace.

Big Freddy was hot on his heels but soon got winded and gave up. Thomas did not trust his luck though, and decided it would be a good idea to hide out for a while and catch his breath before proceeding home. There is a bridge that crosses a narrow creek on East Mockingbird Lane and Thomas took refuge underneath it. He sat for a while out of sight in the shadows, listening to the cars go overhead, great clouds of fogged breath rushing from his mouth. He felt his body slow down and determined it was safe to make the last dash to safety. Then he heard it: a tiny, muffled sound coming from a small, tightly knotted burlap sack sitting half in and half out of the creek water. Thomas knew what was in there and what someone had tried to do to it and what would happen if he didn't act fast. He grabbed up the sack and ran like he had never run before. When he reached his yard, he began shouting.

"Grandfather, Grandmother! Help! Help! Someone tried to murder a cat!"

The grandparents hurried Thomas and his dripping sack into the toasty workshop. Thomas sat the sack on a big table in the middle of the room and took off his coat. The cries from the sack were growing more desperate and Grandfather reached out to untie the knot.

"Be careful, Carl," Clara said.

He struggled with the wet burlap and when he felt it loosen he said, "Now stand back, you two. This little cat is bound to be mad, scared, and all manner of things." The sack was opened but nothing happened; Thomas stepped closer to have a look inside and suddenly something dark shot out and eighteen sharp little claws clung on to Thomas's sweater for dear life.

"Will you look at that? Isn't that the sweetest cat you have ever seen?" Grandmother asked. Thomas, who was gently petting the little bundle said, "It sure is loud! Why won't it stop crying?" Grandfather suggested that a bowl of warm milk would do the trick and reached out to extricate the little howler from Thomas's sweater, but the cat hissed at him and dug in even stronger.

"Looks like he has attached himself to you, Thomas, in more ways than one," Grandfather said. "Carry him on into the kitchen."

After inhaling a bowl of milk and performing an ungrateful act on a bathroom rug, the cat lay curled up on Thomas's lap, purring happily. There was no question of what to do with him and Thomas was very grateful for that; he had never wanted something as badly as he wanted that cat. And it was obvious to all that the cat felt the same way about him! Grandmother called the veterinary clinic in Hillside Village and before he knew what had happened to him, the cat had been weighed, had his temperature taken (he did NOT like that!), and been given his first round of shots (he did NOT like that, either!). The doctor determined him to be about a year old, quite underweight, with some signs of mistreatment but otherwise healthy. The nurse gave Thomas some booklets outlining how to take care of a young cat.

"Now, he has had a rough time, Thomas," she said, "and he is going to be a little skittish. The best way to show him he is safe and loved is to let him adjust to his new home at his own pace. Once he sees he has nothing to be afraid of, he will be all over you with affection."

Thomas promised he would take good care of him. Grandfather had his checkbook out to pay the bill but Grandmother said, "Hold on a minute. This little kitty needs some things before we take him back home." She steered a shopping cart through the aisles and came back to the counter with a pet carrier, a good supply of cat food, a litter box and a big bag of litter, a selection of catnip toys, a brush…oh, it added up! Some grandparents might have thought all this expense was the height of foolishness, but Carl and Clara had both grown up in the country and they knew what caring for an animal can mean to a child's development. Besides, the cost of a little cat is not much at all compared to a barn full of horses and cows! The bill was settled and an appointment was made for next month's booster shots; just one thing remained before the family could leave with its new member: what name to put on the chart? It came to Thomas immediately. "He is Mr. Dickens," he said. And that was that.

It didn't take Mr. Dickens long to make himself right at home in the big house on East Mockingbird Lane. He displayed a healthy appetite, took right to his litter box in Thomas's bathroom, played with his toys until he was worn out and slept most of the night in Thomas's bed. Sometimes he would get up early in the morning while the house was still asleep and explore; if he lost his way or if he found his food bowl empty he would cry until someone, usually Thomas, came to comfort him. And as you can imagine, all the preparations for Christmas fascinated the curious cat. He was everywhere: in the ribbons, the wrappings, the tags; in the decorations, the lights, the ornaments! Adjustments were made, displays were rearranged, tree ornaments were raised above his reach, and, all in all, Mr. Dickens did little real damage. He stood on Thomas's bed and watched the boy tape stencils to the bedroom windows but when Thomas sprayed the canned snow on them, Mr. Dickens did not like the sound at all and took off down the hallway.

The gumdrop tree on the kitchen counter was the little cat's favorite; he would jump up on the counter, bat at a gumdrop until it fell to the kitchen floor, and then jump down and play kickball with it until he lost it. Then he would go back to the countertop for another. Somehow, Grandfather's bare feet always managed to find the "lost" gumdrops when he snuck into the kitchen for a midnight snack so the tree was moved to a spot that he knew the cat could not possibly reach it. Well, he was wrong.

The day Thomas spent Christmas shopping with his mother was hard on Mr. Dickens. According to Grandmother and Grandfather, all the time Thomas was going from one shop to another: John Cobb's, Toy World, The Book Nook, Volk's, the little cat howled his lungs out and would not be comforted. Even with tuna! But the minute Thomas came in the front door, loaded with packages, Mr. Dickens ceased complaining and followed his boy everywhere, purring loudly.

"That is certainly a one-person cat if I ever saw one," Grandmother declared. "He loves you very much, Thomas."

"I love him, too, Grandmother."

It surprised Thomas to hear himself say that. Declarations of love for his mom and grandparents were one thing, but this was a different feeling. Nevertheless, there was no other word for what he felt; he loved Mr. Dickens with all his heart. The object of his affection was purring at his feet, waiting for his boy to put those packages down and pick him up. Just as Thomas was about to do that, his mother said, "There are more bags in the car, Thomas. Would you go get them?"

"Sure, Mom."

"Be careful not to let Mr. Dickens out. He is right behind you."

"I'll watch out, Mom."

It took some doing, but Thomas managed to keep Mr. Dickens from following him outside.

That night the family settled into Grandfather's big Buick to drive through town to look at the Christmas lights and decorations. Mr. Dickens was not left behind though; he sat happily wrapped in a blanket on Thomas's lap taking in all the sights. This year Grandfather extended his usual route and took his family to see the beauty of downtown Dallas decorated for Christmas. All the way down Main and then back again up Commerce, lighted decorations draped across the streets from building to building; shiny bells and red ribbons brightened the light posts; and all the stores: Neiman-Marcus, Titche's, Sanger Brothers, A. Harris, all of them had brilliant windows filled with animated wonders. There was almost too much to see! Grandfather drove around the blocks four times before everyone decided they had seen it all. Then there was the giant pecan tree covered in lights, and the beautifully decorated homes along Turtle Creek; then a loop around Bishop Boulevard to see the Christmas tree at SMU; then home for hot chocolate. Thomas, with Mr. Dickens curled up beside him, slept soundly that night.

Christmas Eve can be one of the longest days of the year. No matter what you find to do to fill the time, it seems time slows down by half. At least that is what it seemed like to Thomas. The family had had its lunch; his mother and grandmother were busy in the kitchen getting things ready for the party that night; Mr. Dickens was asleep in front of the fire; so, Thomas went out to his grandfather's workshop to see if he could be any help out there. Grandfather's nativity scene was all done. He had already set up the stable and manger that morning; now he was touching up the paint on the big star that would hang from a branch of the red oak tree.

"Everything is all set, Thomas. All I need to do is go to Vickery Feed Store and get a bale of hay. Want to come along?"

"No, I think I'll stay here and finish that jigsaw puzzle I've been working on."

"Okay, but when I get back come on out and help me spread the hay around, will you? I've already put some in the stable and in the manger but I want some more to cover the area where the figures will go. And tonight, I'll need your help when we get home from church setting those up."

Thomas said he would be glad to and went back inside to tackle that puzzle. It was a tough one: five hundred pieces and the first one he had attempted all by himself. There were so many times he was ready to give up and ask for help but then he would find the right piece and carry on. Now it was nearly finished and he was just as proud as he could be. He sat down at the card table in the den determined to fill in a particularly pesky area.

"If I can just figure out these snowmen I'll be all done," he called out to the kitchen.

"That's great, Thomas! Here's something to help you keep up your strength," Grandmother said as she set a tall glass of milk and a plate of Christmas cookies on the card table. It was just at that moment that Mr. Dickens decided he needed to see what was going on and he leapt up before anyone knew he was there and knocked over the milk, spilling it all over the puzzle!

"YOU STUPID CAT!" Thomas screamed. "You ruined it! Look what you've done! Get down! Get out of here, stupid cat!" Thomas was still yelling and the cat was moving fast when Grandfather came in the front door. Mr. Dickens made straight for it and was out and away before Grandfather could react. Thomas was horrified by what had happened; not the destruction of his puzzle, but the loss of his friend. He grabbed his coat and scarf and took off after him while his stunned family stood speechless.

❧

Thomas pushed his way through the cold, thick air. The bleak winter sky darkened and the utter silence of Christmas Eve blanketed the neighborhood. He went past homes where frosty windows glowed merrily as happy families gathered around a warming hearth. He went under the Mockingbird bridge; the creek was frozen solid now. Most of the neighborhood shops had closed early; those that had not had no customers and the holiday workers, girls from Woodrow Wilson High School, mostly, stared out at the empty streets and parking lots and wished the clock would move faster so they could go home. The bakery was open and Charlotte was behind the counter. She waved to Thomas and he stuck his head inside and asked her if she had seen a small cat go by. Charlotte told him she had not seen any living thing for close to two hours. And when she offered him one of his favorite cookies, a walnut raisin, she was surprised when he said, "No, thanks." And it was fresh out of the oven, too!

The sky was heavy and low and it was very cold. The wind carried the promise of snow. And to those who ventured outside, it also carried the small, broken-hearted voice of a small broken-hearted boy crying out the name of a Victorian novelist.

Thomas was at the corner of Mockingbird and Ashford when his grandfather found him. He numbly got into the car and half heard his grandfather tell him how worried about him everyone was; how his mother was on the phone asking neighbors to be on the lookout for Mr. Dickens; how his grandmother had set out bowls of food at the front and back doors…but what Thomas heard loud and clear was that he and his grandfather were expected at the cathedral in forty-five minutes! Thomas had completely forgotten. "We'd better go straight there; I'll call home from the Dean's office and let them know I found you and that you are okay." Thomas was about to say that he was anything but "okay" but decided not to.

❧

The Dean had come up with a way to get more children involved in the Christmas Eve family service. Boys and girls were selected to read the lessons and all the children would gather at the steps to the altar to listen to the Dean read the Christmas story from chapter two of the Gospel According to St. Luke. Fathers and sons were recruited to be ushers and it was only natural that Carl Matkin, who had been an usher there for years, decades really, would be their leader and trainer. Thomas and his pals and their fathers were all set to do their parts.

Despite everything, Carl and Thomas arrived in plenty of time; they put on their name badges and stood at their posts to hand out programs. Mae and Clara had stayed behind to prepare for guests and keep an eye out for Mr. Dickens. The service was a wonder! The music, the hymns, the old stone walls and the dark woodwork draped in winter greenery; all splendidly done by many splendid people! Thomas felt as distant from it all as if he were on the moon. He would not talk to his friends; he could not concentrate on his duties. When it came time to carry the wine and wafers to the high altar, Carl gave Thomas's job of presenting the ciborium, a job he had rehearsed to perfection, to Jon instead and told Thomas to follow behind with the collection plates, which he dropped twice while the choir and congregation were singing "Silent Night."

It was indeed a silent night, especially in Grandfather's car during the drive home. But Thomas startled his grandfather by suddenly saying, "When I lived in Amarillo, my dad used to yell at me like I yelled at Mr. Dickens. It always scared me real bad and I would run and hide until I thought he had calmed down."

"You were in a horrible situation, Thomas," Grandfather said softly. "That's why your grandmother and I decided it would be best if you came here to live with us. Your mother, with your help, finally got some good sense and came here too."

Thomas grew quiet again and when his grandfather looked over at him he saw tears in the boy's eyes.

"Thomas?"

"Am I going to be like him when I grow up?" Thomas blurted out. "Will I yell at people and make them scared of me; so scared they want to run away?" The boy was crying harder now and Grandfather stopped the car. He reached out to put his hand on the boy's shaking shoulder but Thomas pulled away and cried, "Well look at what I did today! I scared Mr. Dickens so bad I know I will never see him again! That is just like my dad!"

Carl let the boy cry for a while then said, "Thomas Hardy Godwin, you listen to me. You are nothing like your father and never will be. In the first place, your father would never have rescued that poor cat. In fact, your father would probably have…" Carl caught himself getting a little too heated up and said, "Well, never mind about that. You, my friend, are a good, loving boy. And I know you will grow to become a good, loving man."

"Like you, Grandfather?"

Now it was Carl's eyes that teared up. He hugged the boy to him and said, "Yer darn tootin'! If I have anything to say about it!"

≈

Despite Grandfather's best efforts, Thomas's insides still felt as cold as his outsides when he got home. There had been no sign of Mr. Dickens although both food bowls had been emptied by something. Like he promised, Thomas helped his grandfather carry the big, plastic people and animals from the workshop and set them in place around the stable. Grandfather was adjusting the lights and quietly congratulating himself on doing such a fine job when Thomas went to place the child in the manger. Just as he bent over to lay down the shiny pink plastic Jesus, a ball of fur flew out from beneath the hay and eighteen sharp little claws attached themselves to Thomas's coat! Thomas stopped himself from shouting out with joy and surprise and, carefully putting his hands around his cat, walked slowly into his house.

~

Oh, what a Christmas Eve party that was! The story of the cat and the puzzle and the milk and the search was told to everyone. Grandfather added that he suspected the cat had gone straight to the manger and burrowed down into the hay, coming out to eat the food left for him and jumping back into his nest afterwards. Thomas told how he had searched high and low, far and wide for the little cat he proudly introduced to the guests; and every time he told the story, the distance got a little longer and the air got a little colder. Clara whispered to Mae, "Oh, my. Thomas is getting more like his grandfather every day!"

"And isn't that a fine thing," Mae answered her.

Dr. Burns declared Mr. Dickens to be a "handsome and noble beast who displayed vast amounts of fortitude and resourcefulness throughout his harrowing ordeal." Dr. Burns taught English Literature at SMU and talked that way all the time. Glasses were raised, plates were filled and the happiness of that night was complete. When Jon and his parents bade everyone goodnight, Thomas excused himself and went to his bedroom, Mr. Dickens following close behind. It had been a long and exhausting day and Thomas was ready to put a close to it. He brushed his teeth, put on his pajamas and climbed into bed. Mr. Dickens settled down near him, purring loudly. But before turning off his bedside lamp, he reached under his pillows and brought out a comic book. He patted Mr. Dickens on the head and said, "Now, I am going to read you a story I know you will like,"

"Marley was dead: to begin with. There was no doubt whatever......"

CHRISTMAS FROST

The darkness was giving way to light that cold Saturday morning. It was the first of December and Thomas Godwin's thoughts were brightening too as he walked home, his empty Dallas Morning News canvas bags nearly weightless on his shoulders. He felt lucky to have this route that wound through a new area of fines homes on the south side of East Mockingbird Lane. The area was called The Cloisters and every family there subscribed to the paper, paid their bill on collection day and usually gave Thomas a good tip - a tribute to his sure-armed ability to land the paper squarely on the porch. This time of year, his customers were especially generous and Thomas had a respectable sum of money for Christmas presents left over after he settled his account with Mr. Barnhouse, the route manager. As familiar landmarks became visible, Thomas reached the conclusion that this past year had been the best one of his life. His mother had remained in Dallas after her surprise appearance at the Cathedral last Christmas Eve. She was now teaching sixth grade at Robert E. Lee Elementary and they both lived in the big house with her mom and dad, and that suited Thomas just fine. The adjustments that needed to be made were made easily. The boat rocked only when his father called or sent legal papers. Now all that worry was past. Just one thing remained to be done. There were some things his mother had left behind in Amarillo and she wanted them with her and she now felt brave enough to go get them. She left with Grandfather very early that morning, before Thomas had left to throw his route, and they would be back home by dinnertime.

At breakfast, Thomas and Grandmother planned their day. "It's supposed to rain later today, Thomas. Looks like we will have to find indoor activities to amuse us."

"That's fine with me. My homework's done, all my route collections are paid and I have a stack of comic books waiting to be read."

"You know what else? You could help me crack some pecans and I will bake a couple of pies. Maybe today I can finally get the crusts to come out nice and flakey."

The rain came later that morning and Thomas, sitting on the floor in the den, was glad it was not cold enough to turn to snow. After all, what good was a snow storm if it didn't happen on a weekday and closed the schools? He sat there working on a bag of pecans with a pair of pliers, his pocketknife and two bowls. One bowl was for pecan pieces and the other was for halves that Grandmother would use to decorate the tops of the pies.

"Grandmother, can I ask you a question?"

"You *may* ask me a question, Thomas."

Corrected, Thomas asked, "What do you think happened to make my mom and dad divorce?"

Grandmother removed her glasses and leaned back in her chair. "There were several reasons, Thomas. First of all, your father had a bad war, many of his friends were shot down over France; he himself managed to survive two crashes. He would only talk to your grandfather about it, and your grandfather recognized there was something that had broken and doubted it could ever be fixed. Your grandfather saw it in many of his own men in the first war. Your father had trouble holding a job after the war and was always moving you and your mother from one city to another; of course, that meant your mother would have to find another school to hire her. The pressure on the two of them must have been unbearable; one of them finally had to break."

"What do you mean, Grandmother?"

"Come over here and I'll try to show you. Bring a couple of pecans."

Thomas did as she asked.

"Now hold both pecans in one hand and squeeze as hard as you can, imagine it as the pressure that was pressing down on your parents"

The pecans pressed harder and harder against each other until one of them cracked.

"You see? It never fails. One will go to pieces and the other will remain firm. Your mother remained firm and whole. Am I making any sense to you, Thomas?"

"I think so", he said. "One thing I know for sure is they both could act like a couple of nuts sometimes."

Grandmother's face grew serious. She reached out her hand and felt Thomas's forehead.

"I was afraid of this", she said.

"What?"

"You've got it for sure."

"What have I got?"

"And the saddest part is there's no cure for it. Lord knows I've tried to find one!"

"No cure for what, Grandmother? What have I got?" Thomas's voice rose in genuine concern.

"Your grandfather's unbearable sense of humor", she said and they both broke into long, loud laughter.

   About four in the afternoon, Grandfather's car pulled into the driveway. Thomas and Grandmother were surprised to see them home so soon. His mother had been crying and she looked like she could begin again at any moment. She hugged Thomas and her mother and said, "I'm just tired from the drive. I'll go up and splash some water on my face and lie down a bit before dinner." She went upstairs to her room.

Grandfather was fussing with a box in the trunk of the car and Grandmother asked, "Carl, what happened?"

"Well, it was the durndest thing. We got to Amarillo, found the apartment and, even before we got to the front door, we could see the place was empty. The blinds were up and you could see clear through the front windows to the windows in back. Not a thing in there except for this cardboard box. There was a note on it and Mae read it for a long time, put it in her coat pocket and went back and sat in the car. Not a word to me. So, I picked up the box and put it in the trunk. I thought maybe I had broken something when I set it down because it rattled. I looked inside and boy-howdy! There were the few things Mae had wanted to collect. Bill had done a thorough job on them. Anything that could break, he broke; anything that could tear, he tore. Mae didn't say a word until we were about to Childress. She said it is the book of Mr. Frost's poems that she will miss most of all. Said it was his poems about making the hard choices, which road to travel, and providing for yourself that kept her in one piece during the bad times."

"Oh, dear," Grandmother said, tears in her eyes.

"Now, now," Grandfather hugged her. "The worst is over. She had a good three-hundred-mile cry and she will be fine after a little rest and a good dinner. I'll just set this box in the storage closet and she can decide what she wants to do with it later."

Thomas stood in silent anger. There was nothing he could do about his father's brutal behavior, but he knew now what to get his mother for Christmas.

❧

The following weekend, Thomas was feeling on top of the world. He was getting it all done by himself. At John Cobbs' Drugstore, he had bought some bubble bath and powder for Grandmother and some Bay Rum aftershave for Grandfather. At JoJo's Toys, he had bought a model kit of a Trojan warrior for his best friend, Jon.

"Now for the Book Nook," he thought, "to buy Mom's book and I'm finished."

As he approached the bookstore, he saw a Santa with his bell and black kettle on the corner. He checked his money. He had a ten and a one left. "I can do this. I can give a dollar and still have enough for the book." He strode proudly to the kettle and dropped the bill in. Santa stopped ringing his bell and said, "Thank you, young man. That is very generous!"

"You're welcome," said Thomas. "Merry Christmas!"

"Merry Christmas to you too, my fine fellow!" Thomas was hoping for a "Ho-Ho-Ho", but maybe that was just for children. After all, he was a "fine fellow" and a "very generous young man".

The Book Nook was crowded and Mr. Aldridge, the owner, was very busy. Thomas didn't need any help finding what he came for though; he knew the store well. He found the poetry section and he read the spines. Auden, Byron, Chaucer, Dickinson, Eliot and, finally, Frost. As he reached for the book, a hand touched his and Thomas turned to see a rather large, bearded man scowling down at him.

"Do you intend to purchase that book?" the man asked.

"Yes sir," Thomas answered.

"Well, get on with it then. Aldridge," the man shouted, "do you have another copy of the Frost poems?"

"No, Mr. Griffin, I haven't," said Mr. Aldridge, "and I will not be reordering until after the first of the year."

The large man glared down at Thomas who hurried to the counter to make his purchase and get out of there.

"Will that be all, Thomas?"

"Yes, Mr. Aldridge. It's a surprise for my mother."

Thomas put his money on the counter and Mr. Aldridge said, "You're about four dollars and ninety-five cents short there, Thomas."

Thomas looked at the bill. It was a one. He stared at it for a long time, and realized the mistake he had made at Santa's kettle. "Well, Thomas?"

"Look here. If he is not going to buy the book, I am," said the large man.

Thomas looked up at Mr. Aldridge. "I'm sorry, Mr. Aldridge. I don't seem to have any more money."

"I'm sorry, too, Thomas."

Thomas picked up his dollar and left the store. The Santa and his kettle were gone but he wouldn't have wanted to try to explain the mix-up anyway. As he walked home with his packages, he thought; "If this were television, the big man in the bookstore would suddenly become kind-hearted and rush after me and give me the book." But he knew that that sort of magic doesn't just happen. In real life, it requires a big push and a lot of prayer. He knew what to do.

At home, he hid his packages under his bed and went out to the storage closet in the garage. There was his mother's box and he went through all the broken pieces and torn paper it contained until he found what he needed. Back in his room, he pieced together the title page of the book of poems and wrote the publisher's address on an envelope. On a sheet of notebook paper, he wrote:

> *Dear Mr. Holt,*
>
> *I am writing to you to ask if you could please send me a copy of The Complete Poems of Robert Frost. My mother's copy was torn up by my father and she liked it very much and I want to give her a new one for her Christmas present. She will take good care of it and my father will not be able to tear it up because he lives in Amarillo and we live in Dallas and that is a long way to go to tear up a book.*
>
> *I only have a dollar to send you right now but I will soon have the rest because I have a big paper route and I can start making my collections at the end of the month. Lots of people trust me, and you can too.*
>
> *Yours truly,*

He signed his name and carefully wrote his address. Then he added this p.s.:

> *My mother's name is Mae Godwin and she is a good school teacher.*

The days went by without a response. Thomas was caught up in all the activities that fill the time between the last day of school and Christmas Day itself, but he made sure he was at the mailbox when the postman made his daily delivery. Finally, it was Christmas Eve. His mother and Grandfather were out running some last-minute errands before the shops closed. He stood in his yard and watched. Way down at the end of the block, he saw the postman coming. This was it. The last delivery before Christmas. As the postman neared, Thomas did not recognize him. This was not their usual man, Mr. Howard. The postman came up their walk and dropped a few envelopes into their letterbox and turned to leave.

"Excuse me", said Thomas, "is that all you have for us?"

"That's it, kid," the man said. "Merry Christmas."

Thomas looked through the cards. Nothing for him. Nothing from Mr. Holt in New York. He took the mail inside and put it on the dining room table.

"I'm going out for a little while, Grandmother," he called upstairs.

"Don't be gone long. We'll be going to the Family Service as soon as your grandfather and mother get back and we need to get there early since you are an acolyte again this year, remember?"

How could he forget? Fr. Allen had been rehearsing his acolytes for this night the past three Saturday afternoons. Thomas went out the back gate and walked down the alley. It was very quiet and cold. It was that time on Christmas Eve when everything and everyone waits in quiet anticipation of God's promised gift. The clouds were low and there had been some talk that it might snow. Thomas walked alone with his thoughts.

"Well, I gave it a good try. I'm sure Mom will understand. I can get her the book after my next collection; after Mr. Aldridge gets it in his shop again. This will make a good story - how goofy I was to put my ten-dollar bill into the kettle instead of the one dollar bill. It is pretty funny, but still…"

He came to the end of the alley and rounded the corner of his street. Someone called his name and he turned to see Mrs. Petteway standing on her front porch.

"Thomas, come here," she called.

"Hello, Mrs. Petteway," he said as he climbed the steps.

"Look here, Thomas. That nincompoop of a substitute mailman left this in my door. It's addressed to you."

"My package from New York?"

"No, let me see. The postmark says Vermont."

"Vermont? Who in the world would be sending me a package from Vermont?", he wondered.

"Thank you, Mrs. Petteway," he said and ran home.

He took the package to his room and opened it up. Inside was a letter and another package wrapped in brown paper. He opened the letter and read:

Dear Thomas,

Someone at Henry Holt Publishers forwarded your letter here to me with the idea that I might get a laugh out of it. I did not. Your dilemma moved me greatly and brought back memories of my own childhood.

You may not know this, no reason why you should, but I was raised, along with my sister, Jeanie, by my mother. My father, who was every bit as capable of acts of brutality as I gather your father is, died when I was just about your age and my mother moved us from California to Massachusetts where we lived for a while with my father's parents. My mother was a school teacher like your mother and I loved her dearly and would do anything for her. I suspect you feel the same way towards your mother.

> *Well, enough of this. Don't send me any money, in fact I am returning the dollar you sent Holt. If you are ever around Ripton, Vermont, come by to see me and I will find something for you to do around the farm as repayment. It's the Homer Noble Farm; anyone in town can give you directions.*

Your friend,

R.F.

Thomas untied the string and removed the paper from the other package. There, in his hands, was The Collected Poems. He opened it carefully, a dollar bill fell out, and there, written on the title page in pencil was:

To Mae Godwin,

Merry Christmas from Robert Frost

Dec. 1960

"GRANDMOTHER!!!," Thomas shouted down the hallway.

She shot out of her room. "What is it, Thomas! Good God A'mighty, you've given me the hiccups!" Thomas ran toward her. "Grandmother!" he cried, "do you have any Christmas paper left? Something that's really special?"

THE FIREMAN'S CHRISTMAS

Early morning, before he left his warm bed to throw his paper route, was the time Thomas would think about fathers. Not his own, who had left him and his mother a few years ago and necessitated their move into the big house on East Mockingbird with Grandmother and Grandfather Matkin, but other fathers. He was envious of his friend Ray whose father owned the gas station down the street on Abrams Road; how he longed to be allowed to work alongside Mr. Truelove and sport a red grease rag out of his back pocket like Ray did. Then there was Libby Aldridge whose father owned the Book Nook; Libby always had the first Nancy Drew or Hardy Boys books and her father knew everything under the sun and was a great help with homework. Why, he could tell you when Ben Jonson was born and when he died without looking it up and he could even recite whole poems by Robert Frost right off the top of his head! Best of the bunch, though, had to be Jon's father, Captain Franklin Forrester of Fire Station #17. Oh, boy! To have free run of the stationhouse like Jon did: to slide down the pole, to climb up into the driver's seat and ring the bell, or sit back in the little steering chair at the back of the long ladder. And to be able to do this whenever you wanted to – the thought made Thomas's head spin! Today he would get his chance because today was finally

December 14. It was the last day of school before the long Christmas holiday, the day of the class party and, best of all, the day he and Jon were going to help set up for tomorrow's Open House at the fire station. He jumped out of bed and put his paper-throwing clothes on over his pajamas, buttoned up his Navy pea jacket and adjusted the furry earflaps of his cap before snapping the chinstrap in place. Before he left his room though, he put a big X through the 13th on his John Cobb's Drugstore calendar and smiled brightly at the red-circled 14th. This was going to be a fine day! He nearly collided with his grandfather as he dashed through the kitchen.

"Whoa there, young man! What's the big hurry this morning?"

"I'm ready for this day to get started, Grandfather. I've got a lot to do!"

"Well, the first thing you are going to do is have a glass of this orange juice before you go out the door. Your grandmother will have your breakfast ready for you when you get back from your route."

Thomas drank his glass of juice in one long gulp. "Now, hurry along before you mother sees your pajama pants sticking out of your jeans. You know she doesn't like for you to do that."

"I know. I'll change when I get back."

"All right. Be careful. Don't let the screen door …"

It was too late. The screen door slammed so hard that Thomas's cat, who had been enjoying a morning snooze by the oven, cleared the floor by several inches.

Thomas thought about his grandfather as he walked through the neighborhood delivering his papers. He loved him a lot. Grandfather knew just about everything that a young boy would want to know: knot tying, bait casting, rock collecting – in fact, the man was a walking Boy Scouts Manual!

"But what does he do?" Thomas asked himself.

Every weekday, Thomas saw his grandfather leaving home in a suit and tie and carrying a briefcase. He went to an office in something called the Cotton Exchange. Thomas had no idea what went on there but he was sure it was nothing like fixing a car or putting out fires. In other words, Grandfather was not what Thomas would call "bragging material." Suddenly, Thomas felt ashamed for thinking that way and quickly put his mind to better use.

After the class party, after all the cupcakes and punch and songs and cards, after out-running Diane Larsen who was known to have a handful of mistletoe in her coat pocket, Jon and Thomas arrived at the fire station.

"Hiya, Pops," Jon said.

"Hello, Captain Forrester," Thomas said.

"Howdy, boys!" (Captain Forrester had gone to Texas A&M and said "Howdy" a lot.) "You two ready to lend us a hand?'

"We sure are," Thomas said. "Where do we start?"

"Well, we've pretty much cleaned up the station so, Thomas how about helping the others set up the folding tables and chairs in the dining hall? Jon, you know where we keep the decorations so why don't you take them out front?"

"Okay," the boys said and went about their assignments.

With so many hands the work was done quickly. Soon the fire station was all set: multi-colored lights outlined the roof, brightly painted wooden cutouts of Santa, a sleigh, reindeer, and elves stood in the small yard. Every window was hung with a red-bowed wreath and the corners of the panes were sprayed with aerosol snow. Inside it was just as festive: long tables with red table cloths lined the walls, holly and pine garlands were draped from the ceiling and a magnificent scotch pine decorated with ornaments the neighborhood children had made over the years stood grandly in the center of the hall. Captain Forrester gave each of his decorating crew a cup of hot apple cider and declared the firehouse ready for tomorrow's festivities.

"Good job, everyone," he said.

Thomas saw his mother's car pull up outside so he finished his cider and put on his jacket and cap.

"See you tomorrow, Captain," he said.

"Okay, Thomas. Thanks for all your help and tell your folks I said howdy."

"I'll do that, Captain. Bye."

Jon followed his friend to the sidewalk. "Will it be the same time as usual?" Thomas asked.

"Yep. People start bringing food and stuff around three and the party officially starts at five," Jon said.

"Well, my family is sure looking forward to it so I'll see you then."

"All right. See ya."

❧

The next morning, kitchens were busy all over the Lakewood area. Most folks were preparing the same thing they always brought to the firehouse party but a few brave chefs were forgoing their usual culinary contributions and trying something new. Libby's family had spent Thanksgiving in Santa Fe and she and her mother were making biscochitos and posole. In the kitchen of the big house on East Mockingbird, Thomas's mother and grandmother were a blur of activity. Thomas and his grandfather offered to help but were firmly told that they should stay in the den and work on a jigsaw puzzle or watch The Cisco Kid on television or anything else they could think of – just stay out of the kitchen! It was the same at Jon's house. He was sent outside to split some firewood while his mother made her fruit salad. Strong winds had brought very cold air across Dallas earlier that afternoon and Jon's breath hung in clouds around his head.

Soon it was time to go. Jon carried the salad bowl to the car while his mother locked up the house. "Did you mean to leave the Christmas tree lights on?" he asked her as they pulled out of the driveway. She looked at the glow in the big bay window and said, "Oh, I think it will be all right. I hate coming home to a dark house and just think how pretty it will look after the party."

The firehouse was alive with people. Jon put the bowl down on the salad table and went looking for Thomas. He found him with a group of people who were gathered around a man who was wearing a bright red bow tie that flashed on and off. The man was retelling classic opera stories in such a way that people were bent double with laughter.

"Hey, Jon, come listen to this man. He's very funny! I don't know enough about opera to understand most of it but Grandfather says he has a copy of his book and I can borrow it. He even has a radio show!"

"Well, you know who that is don't you?" asked Jon. "He's Miss Bradford's papa."

"Miss Bradford at the cathedral?"

"The very one."

"How about that? When she gets here I'm going to ask her to introduce me to him."

Others began to arrive: the McShans brought in floral centerpieces for each of the tables, Mrs. Mason and her young ladies from the Casa Linda Bakery set out assorted pies, Mr. White filled one of the tables with all sorts of smoked meats from his restaurant on Gaston Avenue. Thomas saw the Deahls arrive and headed in their direction.

"Don't worry, Thomas, I made your favorite. Chocolate peanut clusters."

"I sure do enjoy those, Mrs. Deahl, thank you!"

"Well, I wasn't sure if we would make it here or not," she said. "We had kind of an adventure!"

"What happened?" Thomas asked.

"It was the funniest thing. We were sitting in the den when that strong wind came through this afternoon. Mr. Deahl thought he heard a strange noise in the chimney and got up to see about it. Well, he opened the flue and this big duck dropped out and came waddling across the hearth and into the room like he owned the place!" She had to stop for a minute to control her laughter and catch her breath. She wiped her eyes and said, "I guess the sudden wind caught him off guard and he fell down the chimney. Well, anyway, we all tried to catch him but he would hiss and snap his bill at us. He was fast too! We chased him back and forth until we were exhausted. Nothing we tried worked—couldn't catch him in a box or throw a blanket over him. Then I had an idea. I got my feather duster out of the kitchen and tied a long piece of string to it and tossed it in front of our visitor. He looked at it and I started to pull it toward me. You won't believe it but he followed that old duster like it was his mama and I was able to lead him out into the front yard!"

The crowd that had gathered to listen to Mrs. Deahl was laughing so hard that they didn't immediately recognize the sudden and deafening sound. But the laughter stopped when they saw the firemen spring into action. It was the alarm bell. One of the men called out, "Dispatch says the address is 7212 Huff Trail, Cap. Isn't that over by where you live?"

"That IS where I live," shouted Captain Forrester, "Let's roll!" The merriment was left behind in a thick cloud of loud noise and diesel fumes.

☙

Jon was too young to be allowed to visit his father at Baylor Hospital so he got all his news from Thomas's grandfather. Jon had become a member of the Matkin household while his mother stayed in the hospital room with her husband. He talked to her on the telephone, but she would get so choked up and sad that he kept their conversations short. When Carl Matkin came home from his daily hospital visits, Jon was full of questions.

"Well, I'll tell you Jon, your dad is going to be okay. If Dr. Percy hadn't been there, his burns would have been a lot worse."

"Someone told me that you were the one who knocked him down and put out the fire that had caught his clothes," Jon said.

"That's true, but Dr. Percy was right there with his emergency bag and got him fixed up until the ambulance arrived."

"Tell me again how it happened, please. I can't quite put it all together."

"All right. Sit down here with me. When your dad and the other firemen left, some of us followed in our cars. By the time we got to your house the firemen were just beginning to hook up their hoses. I

41

couldn't see your father anywhere; then suddenly someone came running out of your house carrying the burning Christmas tree. He nearly ran into me and I tripped him up and covered him with my overcoat. The tree rolled away and soon it and your father and I were hit with the coldest water I had ever felt in my life – it was like cutting a hole in the ice and diving in!"

"What was he trying to do? Why did he run into the house like that?" Jon asked.

"Nobody knows. His crew told me that he leaped off the fire truck before it had even stopped and he broke through the front door without taking the time to put on any protective clothing or gloves. Seems he just wanted to get that burning tree out and away from the house. He's pretty down in the dumps about the whole thing – feels stupid that he had temporarily forgotten everything he had been taught about firefighting. He feels bad too that he used that old string of Christmas lights. He had noticed that the wire around the plug looked a little frayed but he didn't want to take everything down and start all over again."

"What's going to happen with the house. Is it all burned up?"

"Oh no, no! Just that front area around the bay window. There was more water and smoke damage than anything else. The rest of your home is fine."

"But what about the presents? There were a lot of presents under the tree."

"I don't know, Jon, but hey, go round up Thomas. I'm taking us all to Campisi's for dinner."

❧

About a week later, on the morning of Christmas Eve, Captain Forrester was wheel-chaired out of Baylor Hospital and into

Carl's car. His arms and hands were still bandaged and they would take some time to heal but a little of the Captain's old spirit seemed to be returning.

"Howdy, Carl, I sure appreciate you doing all this: letting Jon stay with you this past week and now me and Connie."

"Oh, it's no trouble at all Frank. You're welcome to use our guest room as long as you like."

"It may be a while, Carl. Connie helped me make a few calls about getting the house repaired but it seems that no one can even begin work on it until after the holidays."

"You just set your mind on getting healed up. We'll have a fine Christmas and take care of the rest of it later, okay?"

"Okay, Carl. It's just that Connie and I have never spent a Christmas away from home and I feel bad about spoiling it for Jon too."

"Good God-a-mighty! If you don't stop, I'm going right back to that hospital and ask a nurse to wrap a big bandage around your mouth!"

The rest of the trip down Mockingbird Lane was spent in amused silence. Then, instead of going straight at the light at Williamson Road, Carl turned right.

"Where are we going?" asked Frank.

"I thought we would drive by your house."

"No, I really don't want to see it just yet, Carl."

"Oh, I think you might." Carl turned his big Buick left onto Huff Trail and pulled up about a block away from the Forrester's home. Cars were parked along the curb down both sides of the street.

"Someone must be having a party," Carl said. "We'll have to walk from here." Reluctantly, Captain Forrester got out of the car and followed behind Carl. He knew he would have to face the results of his neglect someday so he set his mind on just getting it over with. There were voices and laughter coming from somewhere up ahead. Frank saw a crowd of people milling around in his yard; swinging their arms and stomping their feet trying to stay warm in front of .... HIS HOME! His home that looked like it had never experienced the destruction of that night.

"What th... Carl, how..." but Carl had joined his family in the crowd. Frank stood there with his mouth gaping and his eyes welling up.

"Will somebody please tell me how...?"

Dr. Percy called out, "We'd be glad to tell you if you would please invite us in before we all catch pneumonia!"

Captain Forrester walked through the crowd of well-wishers. There at his front door stood his wife and son who looked every bit as surprised as he did.

"We just got here ourselves, Frank," said his wife as she put her arms around him. "Thomas's mother drove us over. Mrs. Matkin and her guild from the cathedral are inside. Come see the welcome they have prepared for you!" The three of them walked into the living room followed by their friends.

"How in the world did all this get done?" Captain Forrester asked. "It's only been a week since the fire."

"I can answer that," said Mr. Adams who owned the paint store in Hillside Village, "Matkin worked us like dogs! But to be honest no one worked harder than he did. We had to keep this a secret too and he promised a sorry end to anyone who spilled the beans!"

Everyone who had a part in the rebuilding had a story to tell and Thomas never forgot what he heard that afternoon. How his grandfather had organized a group of men from St. Matthew's Cathedral to restore Captain Forrester's home, how he had gotten merchants and contractors from all over Lakewood to pitch in. Not even the smallest detail escaped Carl Matkin's attention; the presents that were not damaged he repackaged and wrapped, and those that could not be salvaged he replaced. He even managed, so late in the month, to find a handsome Christmas tree for the room and he gave a close inspection to the new strings of lights as he wound them through the branches. Carl knew that the Captain's recovery, both physical and emotional, would be difficult and painful so he made sure that this homecoming would help start the healing. Thomas began to see his grandfather in a new way.

"Your grandfather is a hero, Thomas," Jon said.

"Yeah, I guess he is at that. I had no idea he was doing this. I thought he was just going to his office everyday like he always does."

Captain Forrester made his way to Thomas and said, "I can't seem to find your grandfather. Have you seen him?"

"No, sir. I haven't seen him since we came into your house. Maybe my mom knows where he is"

Only his wife knew that Carl Matkin had decided to spend a little time alone. He was very tired and his hands hurt and he wanted nothing more than to take a slow walk around the neighborhood and enjoy the sharp smell of wood smoke in the chilly air. He knew that there had not been a white Christmas in Dallas since 1926 but the overcast sky looked promising. Carl never missed Dale Milford's weather forecast on Channel 8 and it was a Matkin tradition to watch it on Christmas Eve just before leaving for church.

"Well," he said to himself, "Ol' Dale might have more on his radar screen tonight than just Santa Claus. Wouldn't that be a treat for Thomas!"

For a while he stood watching the darkening sky and thinking about the Christmases he spent as a boy growing up in Corsicana. "Maybe I'll take the family down there next year," he thought. "Thomas should get to know my brother and sisters. Right now, though, I need to get back to the Forrester's."

Late that night, after the party, after the service at the cathedral, Carl Matkin walked through his home making sure that everything was in readiness for the morning. He was glad that Thomas had remembered to leave cookies and milk for Santa. Satisfied, he sat down in his chair by the fireplace, and opened a folded piece of red construction paper that someone had propped against his reading lamp. It read:

Dear Grandfather,

I may never understand what it is you do all week and I may never know what a cotton exchange is, but I do know that I want to grow up to be just like you!

Love,

Thomas.

Clara saw her husband sitting there staring at the piece of paper and asked, "What is it, Carl?"

"The greatest gift any man could wish for," he said.

Carl Matkin kept that card all his long life and he made sure that Thomas never regretted writing those words.

THE HARP

The years Thomas Godwin and his mother lived with her parents in the big house on East Mockingbird Lane were good years. The unconditional loving care of Grandmother and Grandfather Matkin worked its healing magic in an atmosphere of calm safety. Thomas couldn't remember the last time he had the nightmare, the one where his father returns bringing with him more of the old chaos and pain. The horrors of his life in Amarillo were fading. Happiness was not only possible, it was unavoidable!

Christmases past, in addition to the joyous expectations of the season, had brought Thomas's family some unusual challenges. First there was the difficulty of getting his mother to leave an impossible life and start a new one; and the year Thomas had managed to replace a destroyed book that had been his mother's favorite. Oh, and the year of the burning Christmas tree when Grandfather had helped Captain Forrester. Yes, each Christmas had brought a problem that was successfully solved by Thomas and his family. But in 1960 a problem arose that required help from a source beyond themselves. And the change that event brought to one family member was … well, I'm getting ahead of myself.

❧

Carl Matkin was walking across his father's fields in Corsicana one cold winter's afternoon. Now that he was twelve, it was his job to choose and cut down the Christmas tree that would grace the bay window in the front parlor. His father's keenly honed ax rested on his shoulder as he made his way through the softly falling snow. It was easy walking; the snow was barely ankle deep. Soon, however, the flakes got bigger and began to fall harder – up to his shins, his knees! The whiteness was blinding and so thick that Carl could hardly breathe! He dropped the ax and began to thrash his arms wildly trying to dispel the overwhelming whiteness. Suddenly there was a hand on his shoulder and he heard a voice shout,

"Carl, wake up! You're having a nightmare! Wake up!" The "snow" disappeared as Carl's wife pulled the bed sheet away from his face. "Look at you, all tangled up! Here, move your arm. How did you ever get into such a fix?"

"Clara? Oh, my. What a dream! I was out in Daddy's fields and then..."

"Yes, yes. You can tell me all about it later. Now pull yourself together and come down to breakfast, you ol' goof."

She kissed his shiny head and left him there to catch his breath and get his bearings. "Here I am in my own bed in my own house and I can smell coffee and bacon," he said to himself. "I'm sixty-four years old and I have a wife and daughter and grandson living under my roof." When he felt quite sure of these facts, he got out of bed and, by the time he had shaved and showered and come downstairs, he had a plan.

જ઼

"Thomas," he said to his grandson, "this year you and I are going to cut down our own Christmas tree."

Thomas's eyes lit up but Grandmother looked concerned. "Carl, where do you propose to do that? You know we sold your Daddy's land years ago to help Mae go to school down in College Station."

"Yes, yes, I know," Grandfather said, "but there is a place out in East Texas, near Gilmer, where this fella raises Scotch pines. A "tree farm" he calls it. And for a fee you can go out and chop your own. What do you think, Thomas? Sound like a good idea?"

"You bet, Grandfather! When will we go?"

"Well, I've got a few things to do down at the office but I can get away after lunch and we will hit the road if it is all right with your mother."

"Oh, it's fine with me," Mae said, "Momma and I have a lot to do for tonight's party and I'm sure Thomas would love to get away from the house for a while, wouldn't you sweetie pie." Thomas ducked but not fast enough; her arms were around his neck and she gave him a big, loud kiss on his cheek. "MOM!" he protested.

❧

By the time Thomas and Grandfather passed through Mineola, Mae and Clara had finished their errands. They were driving down Williamson Road from Mockingbird, enjoying the bare trees and the soft winter sky when Clara said, "You know, I'll bet there is not a prettier road anywhere in any season than Williamson."

"I agree," her daughter said. "It always looks like one of Daddy's jigsaw puzzles."

"Well, whoever designed this road must have been thinking of jigsaw puzzles – all these twists and turns and sharp corners."

"And the street name changes – Williamson becomes West Lawther and West Lawther becomes White Rock and White Rock becomes Winsted before ending at Garland Road. But I guess that's part of its charm."

"I'll tell you something; this road used to remind me of you when you were living in Amarillo – not sure who you were or what direction you wanted to go."

"Oh, mother. I am so glad that time is over."

"Me too, honey, me too."

They drove to the Casa Linda Bakery for some of Mrs. Mason's pies then on to McShan's Florists for a centerpiece. Before returning home, Mae pulled into the gas station on the corner of Buckner and Garland. The owner, Jim Smith, and a couple of uniformed attendants were quick to leave the comfort of the heated office and offer their services.

"Fill 'er up, Miss?"

"Yes, please," Mae said.

Mr. Smith came around to the passenger side and said, "Well, howdy Mrs. Matkin."

"Hi, Jim. How's business?"

"Couldn't be better! People come from all around to see the big, red flying horse up there on the roof and this intersection is starting to attract some businesses."

"Well, I'm glad to hear it but I think most people come to your station because of you. You sure live up to what your sign says over there – 'the friendliest, most honest and best service station in Dallas.'"

"That's very kind of you, Mrs. Matkin. I plan to keep it that way as long as that horse sits on top of my building."

"That will be a long, long time I am sure Jim."

The attendants finished their duties and tipped their hats. One of them, a tall, red-cheeked young man, tapped on Mae's window and shyly handed her a small candy cane wrapped in cellophane. Mae blushed and was about to thank him but he had run back into the station's office where he peeked at her through the foggy window.

"Thanks again, ladies," said Mr. Smith. "And Mrs. Matkin, you tell that scalawag husband of yours that I know he is trading at Raymond Truelove's but if he will come by and see me I will treat him to a donut and coffee at that new Southern Maid shop they put up across the street."

"I'll tell him, Jim. My best to your family."

As they made their way home, Clara said, "I hope your father checked the gas gauge on his car. He is the world's worst when it comes to paying attention to that." Mae didn't hear; she was thinking about the tall, red-cheeked attendant.

"Well, here we are," Grandfather said as he eased his big Buick through the gates of Tracy's Tree Farm.

"Howdy, fellas," said Mr. Tracy. "Y'all here for a Christmas tree?"

"You bet," said Thomas. "And we brought my great-grandfather's ax to cut it with."

"Whoowee! That's a beauty, and sharp too. You be careful with that. It's just tree limbs you want to cut, not human limbs!"

"Oh, we'll be careful all right. My Grandfather's quite a woodsman."

"Well, choose any tree you like. They're all the same price, two dollars." Grandfather gave Mr. Tracy the money.

"Thanks. Say would y'all mind closing the gate when you're

through? I need to leave here in just a little bit."

"Be glad to," said Grandfather. "I hadn't notice how late in the day it is."

"That's all right. You two just take your time and get a good tree. Merry Christmas to ya!"

"Merry Christmas to you too, Mr. Tracy."

The winter shadows were lengthening as Grandfather and Thomas wandered among the fragrant trees that dotted the gentle hills.

"This one looks good, Grandfather."

"Well, stand there next to it and let me see. No, not quite tall enough."

"How tall do we want?" Thomas asked.

"According to a story I just read in one of your grandmother's magazines we want one that's twice as tall as you."

"What story is that, Grandfather?"

"It's by this fella named Capote and in it he tells of a special Christmas he shared with his aunt in Alabama. In one part the boy, who is your age and called Buddy, and his aunt, who is even older than me and is named Sook, go in search of a Christmas tree. Aunt Sook tells Buddy that the tree should be twice as tall as a boy so he can't steal the star on top."

"Would Buddy have stolen the star if he could?"

"No, I think his aunt was just teasing him. But read the story when we get back home. I have a feeling you will really like it."

The pair trudged through the tree farm, inhaling the bracing scent of all those pines and then Thomas said, "Look here, I think this is the one."

"I fully agree. Yep, it looks to be twice your height. Now stand back while I swing this ax."

Grandfather deftly felled the pine and they carried it back to the car and tied it securely to the roof. It was dark by the time they shut Mr. Tracy's gate and drove down the dirt road that led to the highway. They had driven a couple of miles when the engine sputtered and died.

"Oh for corn's sake!" Grandfather exclaimed. "We're out of gas."

"What are we going to do? Do you have any spare in the trunk?" asked Thomas.

"No, I put that in your mother's car. Don't know why. She NEVER runs out. Oh, your Grandmother is going to have a laugh about this. Now how in the cotton-bloomin' world are we going to get home?"

After some thought, Grandfather decided that the best, and only, thing to do was to walk to the highway and hope someone would give them a lift to the nearest gas station. He figured it was another four miles down the dark road and he was already worn out by his earlier exertions.

"Well, let's put one foot in front of the other, Thomas, and we will get someplace sooner or later."

The pair walked through the cold night. Thomas began to worry about his Grandfather; he was walking slower and breathing harder.

"Are you okay, Grandfather?"

"I'm mighty tired, that's for sure, but let's keep going. The highway should be just ahead."

Thomas listened hard for the sound of traffic but there was not a sound to be heard. Suddenly, he did hear something.

"Grandfather, do you hear that? It sounds like a banjo or violin or something."

Grandfather said, "I don't hear a thing but I do make out some light through those trees. Look here, there's a path leading up there." As they followed the rutted path up the hill, the sound became louder.

"It's a harp, Thomas. Who in 'tarnation would be playing a harp way out here?"

They came to a clearing and there before them was what once had been a fine home. A lamp shone brightly through the front parlor window and they could see a young blonde girl sitting by a fire and playing a harp. As they neared the house, the girl stopped playing and stood at the window with her arms opened wide in welcome. Grandfather was on his last legs when he reached the door. It was opened by a grizzled old man.

"Who in the world is out walking around on a cold night like this?" he asked.

Grandfather was too out of breath to talk so Thomas said, "We ran out of gas back there and were walking to the highway when we heard the girl playing the harp."

"What girl? What harp? But never mind and come on in. You don't look so good," he said to Grandfather.

Warmed by the fire and by the coffee, Grandfather regained his spirits. There were no signs of a harp or a girl anywhere in the large room and he decided it might be best to not bring it up again. After all, the old man, whose name was Argyle, claimed to have lived alone there for nearly forty years and it would be bad manners to question his insistence that they only imagined hearing the music and seeing the young lady.

"When you feel up to it I'll drive you back to your car. I've got enough spare gasoline to get you to Mineola. You can fill up there and call your wife. They haven't stretched the phone lines out this far yet."

"I can't thank you enough, Mr. Argyle," Grandfather said. "Truth is, I'm feeling better than I have in quite some time. I suspect that there was more than coffee in my mug." Mr. Argyle just winked, "Let's get you headed for home," he said.

Mr. Argyle would not accept any money from Grandfather. He did make him promise, however, that he would not get himself in such a fix again. "You're no spring chicken, Matkin. And unlike me you got folks who depend on you. So, take care of yourself."

As he and Thomas neared Mineloa, Grandfather made a mental note to get an appointment with Dr. Percy. There had been an odd pressure in his chest just before he and Thomas had reached Argyle's porch. Probably nothing, he told himself, but still if we hadn't found that house there's no telling what would have happened.

"You're mighty quiet, Thomas. You barely spoke a word at Mr. Argyle's."

"I'm just thinking about that girl. I know we saw her. You saw her, didn't you?"

"Thomas I was so tired I'm not sure what I saw."

"Well, I wasn't a bit tired and I saw her as plain as day."

"Let's just keep that part of our adventure to ourselves, okay? If I start telling about a mysterious, life-saving, disappearing girl with a harp, your grandmother might think I am off my rocker."

"She thinks that anyway, doesn't she?" Thomas asked and grinned.

"Sure she does, but I don't see how it would benefit me to give her further proof!"

Thomas settled back in the Buick's big seat, comfortable and warm and happy that Grandfather was sounding like his old self again. He dozed peacefully and the next thing he knew the big car was pulling into the driveway of the big house on East Mockingbird. Thomas's mother and grandmother and all the party guests came rushing out of the front door, all asking questions at once. Soon everyone was assured that all was well with the two latecomers and a couple of the men, Franklin Forrester and Mike Cline, carried the tree into the living room.

"This tree is a mite cooler that the one you were carrying around in your front yard last year, isn't it Forrester?"

"Cline, one more crack like that and I might forget you are a police lieutenant and pop you one." The laughing men settled the tree into its stand and the decorating party began.

The lateness of the hour did nothing to dampen the spirits of the guests. Indeed, the relief they all enjoyed after so many hours of worry seemed to heighten their jollity. Thomas was famished and he made his way through the crowd to his grandmother's dining table that was groaning under the weight of all his favorites. There was ham and roast and turkey. There was Wanda Smith's famous white potato salad and Mrs. Petteway's green beans with almonds. There was Mary Jane's rolls and Miss Bradford's ambrosia salad. Oh, and the desserts! Mrs. Percy's rum cake (Thomas was allowed a small slice), Mrs. Cline's baklava and, uh-oh did she forget?, no, there they are -- Susan Deahl's chocolate peanuts! Thomas got as much of everything as he could on a paper plate and went in search of an empty chair. His best friend, Jon, appeared through the crowd and asked, "What happened out there in Gilmer? I was sure worried."

"Let's go back to my room and I will tell you all about it – or as much as I understand. There's one part that is mighty strange," Thomas said.

&

Three days later it was Christmas Eve. Thomas and Grandfather had not talked to each other about the girl and her harp but each had given her considerable thought. Thomas was convinced that what he had seen and heard that night had been real; Grandfather fought hard to dismiss it as being the result of exhaustion even though the girl and her harp had probably saved his life. "I'm too old to start believing in that sort of spiritual mumbo-jumbo now."

As the family made its way up the steps to the Cathedral for the Family Service, they overheard Joyce Sneed loudly giving her opinion of the new Dean to everyone within earshot.

"Well, if you ask me he is much too young to be a Dean and furthermore I understand he has a passion for martinis and expensive cigars."

Grandfather, who loved to deflate pomposity wherever he found it, said, "Sounds like my kind of fella! St. Matthew's could use a Dean that understands the needs of the body as well as the soul. Don't you agree Miss Sneed?" Miss Sneed turned her icy glare at Grandfather and didn't say another word.

The Cathedral was decorated in its usual overwhelming magnificence. Dean Michaels, despite his youth, gave an impassioned sermon on the mysterious gift we celebrate at Christmas. As the family stood in line awaiting Holy Communion, Thomas saw something that made his heart leap. Near the top of the piece of stained glass behind the altar there was a figure with golden hair. The figure's arms were opened in a gesture that Thomas recognized and the hands held a banner that read "Alleluia." The line moved closer to the altar and

57

Thomas was sure. He tugged his grandfather's sleeve.

"Look up there! It's her! The girl we saw!"

"Thomas, calm down." Grandfather whispered. "It's just a piece of glass. Now be still." But as they made their way closer, Grandfather found himself staring at the figure. He blinked hard and looked again.

"It can't be. It just can't be," he said softly to himself.

Even as he took communion his eyes were locked on the figure. Before stepping down the chancel steps he turned and looked again as the choir burst forth with "Angels We Have Heard on High." After the service, families hustled and bustled to their cars in the cold night air. In the parking lot Grandfather gave the car keys to Mae and said, "Here, warm up the car for me, please. I have to go back."

"Carl, what's wrong?" Clara asked.

"Nothing, I just forgot something. I'll be right back."

Grandfather made his way into the darkened Cathedral and stood at the altar rail. He looked up at the figure and said softly, "It can't be, can it? But might it be?" Carl Matkin then experienced a lightening of the heart and he thought he might faint. At that moment, all doubt vanished. He stood tall and looked directly into the figure's eyes.

"Thank you kindly, Miss," he said out loud, "for helping me and my grandson." When the figure briefly glowed in the dark window, he knew better than to think it was only his imagination.

A TRUE COMMUNION

FAAAAAAST!!!!! Man, this bike is fast! These were Thomas Godwin's thoughts as he flew through the frosty late October air. The bike was a style known as an English Racer and to make its origin clear to anyone who stopped to admire it, the manufacturer had engraved a map of England on the curved handlebars. Thomas was staring at that map now, imagining he was on some noble quest, ridding the countryside of villains and varlets. In fact, he was doing nothing as exciting as all that, merely finishing up his after-school delivery of The Dallas Times Herald. But his class at Lakewood Elementary was studying King Arthur, and those tales of Arthur and his gallant Knights of the Round Table fired Thomas's blood as nothing had before and sent his imagination spinning as fast as the spokes on his bicycle's wheels. He had even named his gallant black bicycle Llamrai, after Arthur's brave steed.

"Readest ye all about it, Professor!" he shouted as he threw a paper to Dr. Sylvest who had just arrived home from the theology school at SMU.

"Readest ye, Thomas?"

"I'm studying King Arthur, Professor"

Dr. Sylvest caught the paper in one hand and said, "Oh. Well then, thanks Sir Thomas. Good throw!"

Thomas took great pride in his ability to get his customers' papers on their porches, even when traveling so fast astride Llamrai. Sometimes he did miss and he would have to dismount and retrieve a paper from a hedge, but not often. There was one house however where he made an extra effort to land it squarely on the porch: Mr. Cody's. Thomas's route manager, Mr. Barnhouse, had left a note with Thomas's newspaper bundles that told the boy about a new customer. The note gave the address and indicated that Mr. Cody wanted to receive the paper seven days a week, the usual information, but Mr. Barnhouse had added a warning: "Mr. Cody expects his paper to be on time and on his porch each day. He threatens to deduct the cost of any paper that is late or any he must go into his yard to find. Mr. Cody is some kind of "Big Shot," so be careful Thomas."

Thomas made a point of meeting his new customers so on the day he got the note he leaned Llamrai against a tree in Mr. Cody's yard and ran up to the porch. Mr. Cody was out of his front door in a flash!

"Get that bicycle off my tree!" he yelled. "Who do you think you are, damaging a man's tree and trespassing on his property?"

Thomas made a hasty retreat and put the bike against a telephone pole on the parkway but walked back to Mr. Cody, newspaper in hand.

"I'm sorry, sir," he said, "I'm Thomas Godwin, your paperboy. I just wanted to introduce myself."

The old man snatched the paper from Thomas and snarled, "I'm not interested in knowing you, sonny. All I want from you is good service. And if I don't get it, well you'll sure regret it! Now git!"

Thomas was careful and for over a year there had not been any complaints from Mr. Cody; the full amount was always in an envelope stuck in the screen door when Thomas made his monthly collections. The whole block was wary of Mr. Cody; if you let your yard go more than a week without mowing it or if your sprinkler got water on his driveway, you were quick to hear about it! If your kids made too much noise or cut through his yard, he was at your door threatening to tell the state that you were an unfit parent. But no one took the old man seriously; they figured that something awful must have happened to him at some time in his life that made him so obnoxious.

❧

Darkness was falling fast by the time Thomas had thrown his last paper, but he decided he had time to stop at the 7-11 in Lakewood and look to see if any new comic books had come in. The front of the 7-11 was crowded with hay bales and pumpkins and tall stalks of sugarcane but Thomas found a spot for his bike that was out of the way of the front door. The warmth of the store was inviting but the fellow behind the counter was not. It was Fred Slack, a senior at Woodrow Wilson High School who had a bad attitude about having to work while his pals were out looking for trouble. Thomas almost turned around and left but since Fred was busy he decided to try and make his way over to the comic book spinner rack without being seen. No such luck. Thomas was just reaching for the latest Batman when Fred bellowed, "Hey, runt! The library is two blocks that way! If you ain't gonna buy it, don't touch it!"

Thomas withdrew his hand and walked toward the door. He thought about telling Fred that he was surprised that the big oaf knew where the library was but decided against it. Outside, Thomas immediately felt something was wrong. He was looking right at the space where he had left Llamrai but it took his mind a couple of seconds to realize that the bike was gone! He was rooted to the spot, just staring, when Fred came out shouting, "And tell your dumb friend Jon the same goes for him! Don't come hanging around here unless you're gonna buy something!"

Thomas didn't move.

"What's wrong with you? Beat it, I said!"

"My bike's gone," Thomas whispered in disbelief.

❧

Thomas did not remember the long walk in the dark cold air,

he just remembered the blast of warmth he felt when he opened the front door to the big house on East Mockingbird Lane and the blast of voices all asking the same question in various ways.

"Where have you been, Thomas? It is nearly eight o'clock! Your grandfather is out driving your route trying to find you!"

"I'm sorry, Mom, Grandmother," the boy said to the two worried women, "Llamrai was stolen at the 7-11 and I walked home."

"Why didn't you call us Thomas? We were worried sick."

"I would have, Mom, but that bully at the 7-11 was laughing so hard and calling me names that I just wanted to get home as fast as I could."

Finally, his tears came and Thomas was engulfed in the women's arms.

Llamrai was never found. Despite the best efforts of Grandfather, Captain Forrester at the fire station, Office Cline who patrolled the Lakewood area, and all of Thomas's friends, the theft remained a mystery. As Grandfather was driving Thomas to school, a few days after the disappearance, he said to the unusually quiet boy, "Thomas, there is only one practical thing to do. We need to get you a new bike. You need one to get you to and from school and your paper route is too big for someone on foot. It's taking you longer and longer to get that done every day."

"I know, Grandfather. But I will save my money up and get a bike when I can."

"Won't you let me help?"

"No, thanks. I am beginning to believe what that boy at the 7-11 said about me being stupid. It's my fault the bike is gone and it is my job to replace it."

"Now wait a minute. Your bike is gone because some no-account lowlife decided to steal it. Don't blame yourself."

"Well, I sure made it easy for him, just leaving out there."

"Things are changing in our neighborhood, Thomas. Officer Cline tells me that Mrs. Petteway's house was broken into while she was shopping at Volk's and Mr. Speck's car was stolen from his driveway. He had run back in to his house to get something and had left the car running. Sure enough, it was gone when he came out. In broad daylight, in Lakewood! Now people are installing all these new anti-theft devices. I can remember when the only buildings that had bars and alarms on them were jails and banks. But, here we are."

Grandfather pulled up to the school and Thomas gathered up his books. "Have a great day at school. And Thomas, don't let the thief steal more from you than he already has."

"What do you mean, Grandfather?"

"Don't let him steal your belief that, ultimately, goodness prevails."

"I know, Grandfather. Even King Arthur had bad things happen to him but he kept on being King Arthur. He had to; too many people were counting on him. I'll see you this evening."

Grandfather was confident as he drove to his office at the Cotton Exchange that Thomas would slay this dragon that had entered his young life and overcome the heart-hardening effects of someone's crime.

Thomas did his best to serve the many people who were counting on him, his customers. He figured that if he saved every cent he made he would have enough to buy a new bike by summer. But the route was indeed proving to be too much for someone on foot. He had been given such a large route because he had proven to Mr. Barnhouse that his speedy bike could cover the area quickly. Now Thomas was getting home later and later and complaints to Mr. Barnhouse were growing. Finally, at the end of November, Mr. Barnhouse had no choice but to call Thomas and tell him that he was giving his route to a high school boy who drove a car.

"I'm sorry, Thomas, but one of the loudest complainers is that Big

Shot, Mr. Cody, and for some reason the higher-ups at the Herald jump when he speaks. So please understand this is not my idea. I think you were doing a fine job under the circumstances, but my bosses are making me let you go."

"I understand, Mr. Barnhouse."

But as he hung up the phone, Thomas felt as if all the air in his chest had been sucked out and he knew that he really did not understand at all.

When Grandmother heard about Mr. Barnhouse's call, she hit the ceiling (something the gentle woman rarely did) and told her husband, "Carl Matkin, you go out right now and buy that boy a bicycle! Right now, right this minute! I've never heard of such a thing – firing Thomas!!! Well, that Mr. Barnhouse will find out that he has lost the hardest worker he ever had!!! Just wait until I see Emma Barnhouse at the bake sale this afternoon!!! Oh, will she get an earful from me!!!

Grandmother's explosion caught Grandfather by surprise and he spilled his coffee all over his crossword puzzle in a jerking fit.

"Now, Clara," said Grandfather. "Calm yourself. You know I've tried to reason with Thomas but he is stubborn. He won't accept any help at all. I've even offered to let him pay me back when he can, but no, he won't hear of it! Insists that it is his fault the bike is gone and it is up to him alone to replace it. Even offering to get him one for Christmas didn't work!

"Well, we've got to do something. I've never seen Thomas so down in the dumps."

"I'll tell you what I think we ought to do, we ought to let him proceed as he sees fit. I've got to admit I'm rather proud of the way he is taking responsibility; not many boys his age would do that, you know."

"Oh, I suppose you're right. Mae and I will keep him busy with Christmas preparations and he will cheer up and be his old self again in no time."

"That's the spirit, Clara. Nobody loves Christmas like Thomas!"

$\approx$

They were right! Thomas threw himself into Christmas like never before! Even on the first day of his long school holiday, Thomas was up and ready with the rest of the house. He would build a fire in the den and sit down to breakfast with his family and help plan the day. This morning his mother said those words he loved to hear, "I have a lot of shopping to do after breakfast, but you can't come with me Thomas."

"Well, we have some shopping to do too, Mae, and you can't come with us. Right, Thomas?"

"Right, Grandmother."

"How about me?" Grandfather asked.

"No, you can't come either, Carl."

"Well, that's fine because Thomas and I have places to go tomorrow and neither you nor Mae can come."

These were Christmas mysteries that thrilled Thomas right down to his toes! Oh, the days were a whirlwind of activity! Trips to John Cobb's Drugstore, JoJo's Toys, Sanger-Harris, Titche-Goettinger, Woolf Brothers, James K. Wilson, Cullum and Boren, Cokesbury Bookstore and of course, Casa Linda Bakery and McShan's Florist. All this interrupted only by stops at Raymond Truelove's to fill up the car and Charco's or Goff's to fill up the stomach. This year Thomas and Grandfather started a new tradition: Thomas got dressed up in a suit and tie and his mother dropped him off at the Cotton Exchange around lunchtime. There he met some of Grandfather's associates in a round of handshaking and back patting and hearing what a fine young man he is. Then he and Grandfather walked down Harwood to Commerce and turned right a few blocks until they stood before Neiman-Marcus. The store windows were like nothing Thomas ever imagined: animated, life-size characters from A Christmas Carol danced and twirled and flew through constructed scenes. Inside the store, it was just as breathtaking: decorated trees and bright lights and brilliant colors in constant motion. As they passed through the Men's Department, a very pretty girl sprayed Grandfather and Thomas with a men's cologne called Aramis and that made Thomas feel very grown up. Up the elevator the two fragrant men went to the sixth floor for lunch in The Zodiac Room; it would take a dozen Charles Dickens to describe all the luxurious sights and smells that met them! Thomas piled his plate high at the buffet and went back for seconds of a spongy, citrus dessert.

"You like that, do you?" asked Grandfather.

"I'll say! It is like eating a cloud made of orange juice!"

On their way out, Grandfather stopped Thomas and pointed to a bearded man who was talking to customers.

"You see that man, Thomas? He is Mr. Stanley Marcus, the owner of this store."

"He looks a little like Santa Claus."

"Well he sure has been a Santa Claus to Dallas. He is very kind and generous, just a good man. I can't imagine what this city would be like without Mr. Stanley. It wouldn't surprise me one bit if we erected a statue of him right in the middle of town someday."

Finally, everything that needed to be done was done and the family could relax at home and enjoy the few days left before Christmas. Thomas and Grandfather completed a thousand-piece jigsaw puzzle, Mae and Grandmother baked for the Matkin Christmas party. When Thomas learned that the party was on the night of the 24th he sensed something was wrong.

"What about the Christmas Eve service at the cathedral?"

"Well, Thomas," said his mother as she took a cookie sheet of toasted walnuts out of the oven, "your grandfather took it upon himself to write a letter to the newspaper that made our bishop angry. The bishop had the new dean of the cathedral send an answer to the newspaper and that made your grandfather mad at the dean and now the dean won't speak to your grandfather. So, in the spirit of 'Peace on Earth,' he has decided we will stay home this year."

"Sounds confusing."

"It is, dear. Don't trouble your grandfather about it; it just upsets him.'

"I won't, Mom." Thomas said as he helped himself to a hot walnut.

≈

On Christmas Eve, the big house on East Mockingbird Lane was packed with friends and family: Mrs. Petteway, Mary Jane Tracy and the Larsen sisters, Mrs. Dodd and her two daughters, Mike and Helen Cline, Professor Sylvest, an endless parade. Thomas greeted each and every one as he made his way to the dining table to see if his favorites had been brought this year. Yes, they were all there! Wanda Smith's famous white potato salad, Helen Cline's baklava, Susan Deahl's chocolate peanuts, everything seemed to be there. And coming through the door were Dr. and Mrs. Luecke with one of their wonderful rum cakes followed by Miss Dolores Bradford and her ambrosia salad. Thomas loved her salad but the true gift Miss Bradford brought to the party was her father. He was the funniest man Thomas had ever met and here he was in a bright red vest and a green bow tie and filled with more stories and jokes than you can hear in a lifetime!

Thomas's best friend, Jon Forrester, arrived with his mother and father and the two boys made a place for themselves and their loaded plates in front of the television to watch "Mr. Magoo's Christmas Carol."

"I can't wait until tomorrow morning," said Jon. "I hope I get the Mark Wilson magic set I have been begging for since last summer!"

Thomas already knew he would, he had seen Mrs. Forrester buying it at Cullum and Boren, but he only said, "Yeah, that would be neat."

"You think you might get another bicycle?"

"I really hope not," said Thomas. "I told everyone I would replace it myself when I could."

"Well, they might just get you one anyway. Hey, what's this about not going to the cathedral tonight?"

"Something to do with my grandfather and the bishop and the dean. I don't understand it."

"I don't either," said Jon. "All I know is my dad agrees with your grandfather and we're not going either."

It appeared that many of the others felt the same way since the house hummed with festive activities well past midnight -- a joyous fellowship, a true communion.

    It is impossible to express all the love one has for another with gifts, but the family in the big house on East Mockingbird Lane always gave it a good try. There were constant exclamations that Christmas morning of "Oh, my!" and "You really shouldn't have!" and "This is just what I wanted!" and more "Thank you"s and hugs of joy than you could count. By midmorning it was time to clear away the paper and ribbons and enjoy some breakfast. One of the last things most people think about on Christmas Day is the morning paper but Grandfather was a man of habit and had to have his paper with his coffee and he asked Thomas to get it for him. Thomas opened the front door and was blinded by the sun reflecting off the frosted front lawn. But he did see a car backing out of the Matkin driveway and he thought he recognized the driver.

"But what would he be doing here?" he wondered.

Then he saw it! Coming back from the yard with the newspaper, Thomas saw a new bicycle leaning on its kickstand in front of the porch swing! It was a racer, too, with wire baskets on either side of the rear tire! For a second he thought that a repentant crook had brought Llamrai back, but this bike was brand spanking new! He ran into the house and said, "I can't believe you got me a bicycle after all the times I told you I would take care of it myself!"

He didn't know whether to be petulantly angry or deliriously happy! "What are you talking about?" said Grandfather. "We didn't get you a bicycle. Did we, Clara? Mae?"

Grandmother and Mae both denied knowing anything about it and they all followed Thomas to the porch to see for themselves. "Will you look at that? It is a very handsome bike, Thomas. But I promise you it is not from us," his mother said.

"Look here. There is a card on the handlebars," said Grandmother. "It says 'For the paperboy.' Must be one of your customers, Thomas."

Just then the telephone rang. Grandfather answered it and came back to the group on the front porch.

"It's for you, Thomas," he said. "Mr. Barnhouse."

Thomas picked up the phone in a daze.

"Hello, Mr. Barnhouse."

"Thomas I'm in a real fix and I need you to help me out if you can."

"Sure, Mr. Barnhouse, what can I do?"

"You can come back to work for me! Today! This afternoon! That fella I hired to take your place has been terrible – late deliveries, sometimes no deliveries at all, or papers thrown at the wrong houses. Oh, it has been awful. Mr. Cody has been yelling my ear off with complaints. And now today, on Christmas Day for crying out loud, the fella calls me and quits! Will you do it, Thomas? My boss says I can give you a big bonus if you say yes."

"Yes, Mr. Barnhouse, of course I will. I'll get on it right now."

"Great! Your bundles will be at the old drop-off place – same as usual. Thanks a million, Thomas. And that bonus I mentioned? It's a hundred bucks, Thomas, a hundred bucks!!!"

Thomas leapt into action. He told his bewildered family, "I've got my old job back! Mr. Barnhouse's boss is giving me a bonus! I have to get going! And I will come straight home, no stopping at the 7-11 today!" Not thinking that it would not have been open on Christmas Day anyway. Carl and Clara and Mae could only stand open mouthed on the porch waving as Thomas sped away on the mystery bike.

And speed he did! His side baskets loaded with newspapers, he zipped through the familiar streets. There was Professor Sylvest!

"Ahoy, matey!" Thomas shouted as he threw a paper to the professor.

"Ahoy, matey??? What happened to King Arthur?"

"Oh, I'm reading Moby Dick now!" he called back over his shoulder.

He landed a paper dead center on Mr. Cody's porch at full speed but put on the brakes when he heard the old man shout, "You! Paperboy! You come right back here!"

Thomas did as he was told and asked, "Is there something wrong, Mr. Cody? I'm sorry if there have been problems before but that was someone else, I just started back today."

"I know that. No, no problem today. I just have something to give you, that's all."

He walked to his car, the car Thomas was sure now that he had seen earlier in the driveway at home. Mr. Cody opened the trunk and lifted out a strong steel-link bicycle chain and lock.

"Here. Maybe this will help you hang onto your new bike for a while. I heard about what happened to the other one"

"How…?"

"No questions, now. Just take this and remember to use it."

"You left this bike on my porch, didn't you? I saw you leave in your car."

Mr. Cody bent over and looked into Thomas's eyes, "I'm going to have to have a talk with your family! It would appear that you have been into the adult's egg nog!"

"No, sir. I'm sure it was you and I can't let you do it."

"I'll have you know that there are very few people, least of all a little boy, who can tell me what I can and cannot do, young man."

"At least let me pay you for it. I can, really! I am getting a bonus from the paper for coming back to work!"

"Oh, you'll probably throw that hundred dollars away on comic books and candy and…"

The two stared silently at each other as Mr. Cody's slip-up sank in.

"I never said how much it … You must've told Mr. Barnhouse to …" Thomas sputtered.

"Now look here. It's too cold to stand out here yapping all afternoon. And by the looks of your baskets you still have more papers to throw. People are waiting! Get going!!!"

With that Mr. Cody went inside and closed the door on a mystified Thomas. The interior of the Cody house would have surprised his neighbors. It was bright and cheery, very unlike the gruff old man who lived there alone. In the corner of the den stood what was once a grand Christmas tree surrounded by presents. But the presents had not been placed there recently – they had sat there for more than a year and were covered with the fallen needles of the dried-up Fraser fir. Mr. Cody went to the mantle of his roaring fireplace and stared at a picture of his wife and daughter and grandson. Anger and anguish fought for control of his tired eyes --- but that is another story for another time.

&

One late afternoon about a week later, after he had done a little investigating with the help of Grandfather and after he had received his bonus money, Thomas appeared on Mr. Cody's porch. He handed Mr. Cody the newspaper and said, "I wanted to give this to you myself. Just to be sure you got it. This is strictly a business deal, but I want to say thank you anyway."

"All right, all right. You've said it. Now get those papers delivered!"

Thomas rode off as proud of himself as he could ever remember being. In his imagination, he was rushing full-sail through the high seas in pursuit of the white whale.

"Avast, me hearties! Thar she blows!!!" he shouted.

In his den, Mr. Cody opened his paper. An envelope fell out and the old man sat on an ottoman to examine its contents: a precise number of bills and coins and a bill of sale that read: *"To Mr. Nathaniel Cody, former editor-in-chief of The Dallas Times Herald, payment in full for the 'Pequod.'"*

It was signed, *"Thomas, call me Ishmael, Godwin."* A moment passed and then, for the first time in a very long time, Mr. Cody burst out laughing.

CHRISTMAS MOURNING

Carl Matkin rarely visited Willy's Barbershop; in fact, his lack of hair was a never-ending source of humor for those living in the big house on East Mockingbird Lane. It was two days before Christmas and you would have thought that she had other things to occupy her mind, but Carl's wife, Clara, stood behind him as he sat at the breakfast table, ran a napkin over the top of his shiny dome and said, "Hold still a minute, dear, I want to check my makeup." (There were many variations of this loving tease, such as: "If you are going out in the sun be sure to wear a hat; you don't want a low-flying pilot to think that someone is trying to signal him with a mirror!" and "I remember when you had a full head of beautiful, wavy hair. Too bad it was waving goodbye!") But this cold December morning, nothing could disrupt Carl's happiness. It was nearly Christmas and joy hugged every fiber of his being. He was a naturally optimistic and generous man and Christmas intensified that which was most wonderful in his nature. And despite his reflective pate, Carl was a handsome man; tall, slender, with the facial features of a movie star and a semi-circle of thick white hair that grew from his temples all the way around to the back of his head. This snowy wreath needed trimming, it had grown a little long over his ears and shirt collar, and Carl said to his laughing wife, "Well, since you are having such a good time at my expense, here's something that will really send you over the edge."

"What?" Clara asked trying unsuccessfully to control herself.

"I am going to get a haircut this morning," he replied with great dignity.

That did it! Clara's fit of laughter threatened all breakables within the house!

Carl got his coat and long muffler from the hall closet and called back to Clara as he put them on, "I'm going to see if Thomas wants to go with me. We'll walk so you and Mae can have the cars in case you need to do any last-minute shopping." Clara was laughing so hard she could not answer, so she just waved a hand to let him know she understood. Carl found his grandson in the front yard putting the finishing touches on the decorated gaslight.

"Want to walk with me to Willy's?"

"Sure, Grandfather, let me run inside and tell Mom."

"I told your Grandmother already, so let's go before I have to endure another hair joke."

They almost made it out of earshot when Clara shouted to them from the front porch, "You tell Willy that he ought to be ashamed of himself for charging you full price!" Clara's laughter, now punctuated by hiccups, filled the freezing, grey air. Thomas and Grandfather hurried on, bending against the blustery winter wind.

"Once your grandmother gets hold of something she enjoys, she just won't let it go, will she?"

"Well, you ought to be glad of that, Grandfather."

"Why's that, Thomas?"

"She got hold of you, didn't she?"

"Truer words were never spoken, young man. And one day I'll tell you how I managed to make that happen!"

❧

The location of Willy's Hillside Village Barbershop could not have suited Thomas better; JoJo's Toys was on the left and Hillside Bakery was on the right. But it was too cold to stand and window-shop so he followed his grandfather into the defrosting warmth of Willy's.

"Come in, gents, come in!" said Willy, a large, rosy-cheeked man whose abundant hair was as shiny and black as licorice whips. "Help yourselves to some hot apple cider and Christmas cookies. I'll be right with ya as soon as I finish up Cody here."

"Hi, Mister Cody," said Thomas, "Merry Christmas."

Mr. Cody looked older and sadder than Thomas remembered but it had been nearly a year since he had seen him. He wondered if he had been ill. The old man blinked a couple of times and looked at the boy standing by the door but it was clear to Carl that those eyes were seeing something or someone that no one else could see. When Willy finished brushing his neck with talc, Mr. Cody wordlessly paid the man, put on his overcoat and left.

"Brrr. That man carries a winter chill with him all year long," said Willy. "Good tipper, though!"

"There is some good in there somewhere trying to get out, all right. He was especially kind to Thomas last Christmas."

"I heard about that and it surprised me right down to my shoes. Imagine him doing something like that, and at Christmas too. Didn't last long though, did it? He was his old, hateful self by New Year's.

And the closer it gets to Christmas, the meaner he gets!"

Grandfather settled himself into the tall barber chair and said, "Yes sir, this is the worst time of year for him I'm sure." This stunned Thomas, who had been sipping his cup of hot cider and staring at all the brightly colored bottles of hair tonic arranged in front of Willy's mirrors.

"Who in the whole wide world would think Christmas is the worst time of year?" he asked.

"Well, Thomas," said Grandfather, "Mr. Cody suffered a heavy, painful loss on Christmas Eve a few years ago and the memory of that night upsets him terribly."

"What happened that would make him hate Christmas?"

Willy answered, "Oh, I don't think he hates Christmas, Thomas. He just hates what happened and I'm sure all the fun and joy and happiness he sees around him must make his loss seem that much greater."

Thomas hesitated but he had to know; "What did he lose?"

Grandfather took a deep breath and said, "He lost his entire family, Thomas. Wife, daughter and grandson in a car crash."

The bell above Willy's door broke the solemn silence.

"Hi, fellas," said Professor Sylvest.

"Hi, Ed," said Willy. "Come in and warm up. We were just telling Thomas here about what happened to Cody's family."

"Oh my, that was one awful Christmas Eve," said the professor as he helped himself to some cider and cookies. "You know his wife Mary worked for me at SMU. I'll never forget how excited she was when school ended for the Christmas break that year. Their daughter and grandson were coming from Santa Fe and she had found the perfect gift for Cody. Every year she wracked her brain to come up with something really unusual for him, something that would surprise and delight him. Something that would be a reminder all year long of how much she loved him. She told me that seeing the look on his face when he unwrapped it was the best part of Christmas morning for her. In fact, that's what she was doing out in the station wagon that late on Christmas Eve; going with her daughter and grandson to pick up his gift. It was something large and she didn't have a good hiding place in their house so she left it at the store until the last minute."

The professor paused to take a sip of cider, "Never found out what the gift was. After the car went off the bridge, the fire, you know…"

"We don't need to go into any great detail," Grandfather cautioned him, with a quick nod toward Thomas.

The walk home was very cold; there was something in the air that was not quite snow and not quite sleet. Thomas was unusually silent and Grandfather asked, "What's the matter? Do you think your teeth will freeze if you try to talk in this weather?"

"No," Thomas answered, "I was just thinking about Mr. Cody. Grandfather, do you think there are a lot of people like him, people who are hurting so bad that even Christmas can't cheer them up."

"Unfortunately, I think there are quite a few, Thomas. There will be some who will wake up Christmas morning and, instead of gathering around a Christmas tree with family, will be going to sit at the bedside of a loved one in a hospital, or visiting a cemetery to leave a wreath. Some will be sad and angry that for one reason or another they will not be able to see their children, and some, like Mr. Cody, will sit alone grieving over an old loss, feeling cut off from everyone. And then there're the poor and those in prisons; lots of unhappy and unfortunate people."

"I never thought about that," said Thomas.

Grandfather put an arm around the boy's shoulder and said, "Most people don't."

When they came in through the front door, Thomas and Grandfather found the house to be a hive of activity. How two women could be in so many places at the same time was amazing! There was so much to do to have everything ready for tomorrow's Christmas Eve party. Mae told her father and Thomas to keep their coats on because, in addition to everything else that remained to be done, Dr. Wortman had called a last-minute rehearsal of his carolers! The Matkins and their guests were going to do something new this year: caroling through the neighborhood. Dr. Wortman, the choirmaster at the cathedral, had been working with them since the Friday after Thanksgiving and, guided by his professionalism and limitless patience, the group now managed to produce a sound that was less and less like that of a gathering of angry alley-cats and more like "a joyful noise."

Around eleven o'clock, all the carolers were in place in the choir pews. After a quick run-through, Dr. Wortman said he wanted to work with the sopranos and asked everyone else to come back into the cathedral in twenty minutes. The men and boys made their way to the Great Hall where refreshments were offered by one of the guilds. Carl got into conversation with a few of his cronies, Mr. Greiner, Mr. Allspaugh and Dr. Luecke so Thomas wandered over to look in the window of the cathedral bookshop. There were boxed cards, colorful books, golden angels that spun around and struck chimes when you lit the candles, and best of all, a magnificent nativity set. He heard faint music and saw a light coming from someone's office at the other end of the long first floor hallway. Curiosity pulled him to the door where he saw Father King writing at his desk.

"Well, Thomas! What a nice surprise! Come in, come in!" Thomas loved Father King deeply and he gladly accepted the invitation. "Practicing with Dr. Wortman, I take it?"

"Yes, Father. He is taking us caroling on Christmas Eve."

"That's wonderful! 'Here we come a-wassailing' and all that, eh?"

"I suppose," said Thomas.

"Why, Thomas, where are you usual high spirits? You seem a bit glum."

"I learned what happened to Mr. Cody, why he is so unhappy and angry all the time."

"Ah yes. Cody. Very sad story that."

"Do you know Mr. Cody, Father?" Thomas asked.

"I should say I do! The very first marriage I performed as a young priest was his and Mary's. Indeed, I christened their daughter and grandson. And, I am sad to say, I presided at the funeral."

"My grandfather told me that there are a lot of people who are sad and lonely at Christmas. Aren't they ever happy again?"

Father King thought for a moment. "Grief can be a very slow process for some people, Thomas. We must respect their pain and not insist that they feel or act a certain way during the holidays simply because that would make us feel better. One of my favorite authors, May Sarton, put it this way in her wonderful book The House by the Sea; 'We convert, if we do at all, by being something irresistible, not by demanding something impossible.' All we can do is love them and try our best to help them get through a difficult part of their journey."

Thomas asked, "What do you think Mr. Cody would find

irresistible?"

"I don't know, Thomas, but it is my daily prayer that it comes to him before he sinks so deep in his despair that nothing can pull him out."

Thomas heard his grandfather's voice calling him. "I've got to get back, Father King. Will we see you at the party tomorrow?"

"I wouldn't miss it for the world, dear boy! God bless you!"

It was bitterly cold that Christmas Eve when everyone gathered in the Matkin's front yard. Dr. Wortman handed out the music books and led the way down East Mockingbird toward White Rock Lake. The caroling was well received; people peered through their curtains or came out on their porches to hear and thank the singers. House decorations glowed brightly in the darkening twilight as the traveling troubadours made their way up Hillgreen and down Brookcove. One house they encountered, however, was dark.

"That's Mr. Cody's house," someone said. "We might as well move on."

"No," someone else answered. "I see a light coming from somewhere in there. And there is smoke coming out of the chimney. Come on; let's give the old boy our best. What harm can it do?"

Others agreed and they were not far into "God rest ye merry gentlemen, let nothing you dismay..." when they saw the light go out. That didn't stop them, however. They redoubled their efforts. "Angels we have heard on high..." they saw a hand pull the front curtains shut tight. That would have discouraged most people but this little band of carolers was determined to prevail.

Inside the darkened house, Mr. Cody was at war with himself. He had a strong desire to throw his door open and welcome the carolers but he had an equally strong desire to hold onto the twisted idea that somehow it would be wrong for him to enjoy their company without his family there. He looked in the corner where the dried-up, old Christmas tree stood; the presents meant to be opened long ago by those whose faces smiled at him from the picture on the mantle.

"Mary would be ashamed of me if she knew how I have been behaving," he thought to himself. "I have been unkind to most of the people out there on my sidewalk. It felt good to help that boy last year, maybe I can…"

Then he heard the lyrics, "I wonder as I wander out under the sky, how Jesus the Savior did come for to die, for poor ornery people like you and like I…" Suddenly tears shot from his eyes and his chest expanded as if a tight band had been broken. He ran to the door calling "WAIT, WAIT" to the departing crowd. "Come back, please. Oh, come back."

The carolers stopped in their tracks. Alarmed, Carl, Officer Cline and Captain Forrester ran back to the house.

"Cody, is anything wrong?" asked Carl when he reached the shaking man.

Mr. Cody, who was having a fit of laughing and crying, said, "Wrong? No, no, nothing's wrong. In fact, I think life is finally going to be right! Yes, I know it is!"

The others had come into Mr. Cody's yard and watched in amazement as the old grump's face became more and more cheerful. "Come in, please, come in and get warm. Let me get these lights on and put more logs on the fire!" He hurried about the house going from one room to the next stopping often to apologize for his bad manners and shaking the hand of each person. "Come in to the den all of you and let me explain. That last song, that somber carol, was my wife's favorite. She said she found comfort in it and I used to tease her and tell her it was much too morbid to be sung at a festive time like Christmas. But she insisted that I was missing the point. To her the song said that even with the knowledge of death, happiness was still possible! And I stand before you now to declare that it is true. It's true, even for an "ornery" old man like me, IT'S TRUE!"

He stopped to catch his breath and saw the puzzled faces of his guests. "I may not be expressing myself as well as I would like to, I am so overwhelmed by my gratitude. Thank you for coming and singing to me tonight. I wish I had something to offer you…"

Carl spoke, "Mr. Cody, why don't you come with us? We have a feast waiting for us and you are surely welcome."

"Oh, no. I hope you will forgive me. I truly appreciate your kindness, but I, oh I feel silly about this, but I would really rather stay home tonight. I hope you understand."

It was time for Clara and Mae to take over. "Of course we do," said Mae. "But, if you don't object, why don't we bring the feast to you? You certainly have the room!"

It was not easy for him, but Mr. Cody banished a sudden fear of all this excitement and hopefully asked in a whisper, "Would you do that? For me? Are you sure it is not too much trouble?"

"Trouble? Nonsense!" said Clara. She selected several men and women to go with her to pack up and transport all the food and drink at the big house on East Mockingbird. The rest stayed behind and, under Mae's direction, prepared for the party.

Mr. Cody had a concern and he called Carl and Captain Forrester over to him. "Look here, Matkin, I don't know quite what to do with these gifts. They have sat here covered in fir needles for years not doing anyone any good. What would you suggest? I can remember what is in each one of them if that helps."

"Let's load them in your car and tomorrow morning we will take them to the Salvation Army Center. A few men from the cathedral are going there to hand out presents and serve meals this year. Join us."

"That's perfect!" cried Mr. Cody. "And Forrester, don't you think this old tree has become a fire hazard and needs to be disposed of?"

"Yes, indeed it does. Out it goes!" said the fire chief.

Soon that sad corner was cleared and cleaned. And just in time because Clara and her crew were coming through the front door!

Oh, what a parade of delights: Mr. Speck's smoked turkeys, and hams, and brisket; Wanda Smith's potato salad; Jane and Ed Baca's baked breads; Dolores Bradford's ambrosia salad; Marion Luecke's rum cake; Zoe Urbanek's French pastries; Susan Deahl's chocolates; Pamela Patton's Swedish meatballs; and more and more and more! Soon every flat surface in Mr. Cody's den, dining room and living room held gastronomic temptations! Mr. Cody was a whirling dervish among his guests, learning about their lives. Several times he stood on his raised hearth and made announcements: "Ladies and gentlemen, I have just discovered we have with us tonight some men who served in the Civilian Conservation Corps! Let's show our appreciation to them! They made White Rock Lake Park the gem it is today!" The room exploded in applause! Later he called out, "And here is Thomas Godwin! The fine young man who brings us our evening newspaper! And there is his friend Jon Forrester whom I have heard is a fine amateur magician! Will you perform for us, Jon?" More cheers and applause. On and on until Mr. Cody had made all his guests feel proud of themselves for whatever contribution they made to the community. There were songs and jokes and stories; someone turned on the television just in time to see the progress of Santa's sleigh on the Channel 8 weather radar screen and that sent the children into fits of excitement! The Cody house vibrated from its foundation to its rafters with a joy it had not felt for many years.

&

Too soon it was time for everyone to leave, to go to their homes and make the final preparations for the glorious morning that was only hours away. Mr. Cody stood by his front door feeling merrier than he could remember ever feeling and in the flurry of handshakes, hugs and more than a few kisses to his reddened cheeks he thanked his departing visitors and heartily accepted every Christmas Day invitation he was offered. As the last car pulled away, Mr. Cody realized that he was now expected at four breakfasts, five brunches and six dinners! All in one day! He laughed at his foolishness until his sides ached, "But I'll be there! At each and every one of them! Even if I swell up and burst like a balloon!" Then a thought came to him and he stood in the cold, still, silent night and stared at the thousands of winking stars.

"Mary?" he whispered. "You know that gift you were so excited about finding for me? I think it was delivered tonight. Thank you, my love."

THE WRITING CONTEST

Nathaniel Cody was a happy man; indeed, he was probably the happiest man in the entire Lakewood neighborhood. And like all truly happy men, he was truly generous and good hearted. This Saturday morning, the first full day of the school children's Christmas vacation, Mr. Cody's generosity and kindness were on public display at the stately Lakewood Library. It was time for story hour and when Miss Johnson finished reading "The Farolitos of Christmas" to the packed room she asked the children to stay seated for an announcement.

"Boys and girls, I am very excited today. Do you want to know why?" Everyone did. "It's because today I am privileged to announce the first annual Lakewood Library Christmas Story Contest." A low murmur swept through the children. "Mr. Nathaniel Cody, who is here with us today, will give you the details. Mr. Cody." As Mr. Cody stood, Jon nudged Thomas and whispered, "I wondered what he was doing here."

"Shh. Let's listen," Thomas answered.

"Young ladies and gentlemen, I bid you good morning," said Mr. Cody. The children returned his greeting. "I am so happy to see so many of you here on this cold morning. Before I speak about the contest, I would like to thank Miss Johnson for allowing me to come join you today. I must say that you children are very lucky to have such fine librarian in this community. So why don't we all express our appreciation." The room exploded in cheers and applause; Miss Johnson shyly acknowledged the love that was sent her way and held her hands up in a futile attempt to bring it to a close. After everyone settled down, Mr. Cody continued. "Now about the contest. We, I and the other judges, want you to write a story that has a Christmas theme. It should be original, meaning it should be your story and yours alone. I know your parents will want to help you. That's only natural. But be firm in telling them that you must do it yourself. Use your imaginations; be as creative as you can be. And, oh yes, have fun! I am sure I have left out something. Does anyone have a question?"

Hands rose all over the crowded room. "Oh, I see I must have left out a lot! Yes, you there in the pretty red sweater."

"How long does it have to be?"

"No more than 500 words. Yes, you next."

"Can we draw pictures, too?"

"No, we want just your words. I'm sure many of you are very talented artists, but we want to find those of you who are very talented writers. Next."

Miss Johnson whispered into Mr. Cody's ear. "Ah, of course. Miss Johnson has reminded me that a full list of instructions has been printed and that it should tell you all you need to know. You can pick one up on your way out." Miss Johnson whispered again. "Oh, my. I am forgetful," said Mr. Cody. "Miss Johnson tells me that I neglected to announce the prizes!" The children squirmed in delight. "There will be three awards: third prize will be $50, second prize

$100, and first will be $200 and the inclusion of the winning story in the Christmas Eve supplement of The Dallas Times Herald."

Oh, the windows rattled with the burst of astonishment. "Thomas, did you hear that? Two hundred dollars!" Jon was shaking his friend so hard that Thomas's bubble gum flew out of his mouth and landed in Diane Larsen's bright red hair! As he reached to retrieve it, she and her best friend, Donna, rushed toward the front of the room. "Hurry, Donna, let's get the instructions sheet and get started." Thomas lunged after her but Jon held him back. "Let it stay. It's almost the same color as her hair anyway and you can hardly see it." Thomas agreed it might be the best idea.

Miss Johnson called the confusion to order. "Mr. Cody has something else to say before we leave." Mr. Cody thanked Miss Johnson and told the children, "I just wanted to add that you should not write your name on your story. When you turn it in here at the library it will be assigned a number. None of the judges will know who wrote which story. Now, goodbye, good luck, work hard and we hope to see many of you here at the awards party on Christmas Eve morning."

The children bundled into their coats and hats and either joined their parents who were waiting in warm cars in the parking lot or unchained their bicycles and braced themselves for a cold ride home. "Can you imagine that," Jon exclaimed. "Two hundred bucks for just writing a story! Wouldn't it be great to have that kind of money to spend at Christmas time?"

Diane, who had read everything in sight and was very proud of that fact said, "Well, you boys can forget about winning, because everyone knows women are the best writers. Jane Austen, Charlotte Bronte..." Jon shot back, "Whadaya mean? How about Stan Lee, huh? Stan Lee writes "Spiderman" and I bet more people read "Spiderman" than your old Jane Austen!" Irritated, Diane said, "Oh you are such a.... Come along Donna; let's leave these little boys to their comic books. We have some real writing to do."

The group of friends broke up and went their separate ways. Jon was still fuming. "She thinks she's soooooo smart. I wish I could see her when she finds that gum in her hair! Just wait until I win first prize. That'll show her."

"So, you are going to enter?" Thomas asked.

"Of course, aren't you?"

"I guess," Thomas said. "If I can come up with something to write about."

Jon was excited. "I've got a great idea. I'm gonna have Santa Claus kidnapped by some spacemen and his elves will take off in fighter jets to save him! Good, huh?"

"Yeah, that sounds cool," Thomas agreed. "Wish I had thought of it."

"You'll come up with something. Hey, I'll see ya. I want to get home and get started." Jon pedaled away on his bicycle and Thomas was left alone in front of the big library in the cold, grey afternoon wondering where on earth stories came from. He had never really thought about it before.

    As Mr. Cody rode home in his big black car, he thought to himself, "Well, that went very well indeed!" But since the great turning point in his life last Christmas Eve, everything had gone well for the good old man. "I guess this is how dear Ebenezer Scrooge felt after his fantastic Christmas Eve adventure. Mr. Dickens tells us that Scrooge promised to 'honor Christmas in my heart, and try to keep it all the year' and that 'he was better than his word'. And that 'he became as good a friend, as good a master, and as good a man, as the good old city knew, or any other good old city, town, or borough, in the good old world.'" He was still thinking about A Christmas Carol, how he wished Dickens had written more about the rest of Scrooge's life, when he turned onto his driveway. He hung his coat and scarf in the hallway and called, "Well, are we all assembled?"

"Yes, we are in the den," a man answered in a thick British accent.

"Ah, and so you are," Mr. Cody said as he entered the room. "Hello, Ed. Francine. I trust my guest has introduced himself. But of course, you already know him, don't you Ed?"

"Yes, indeed. And I am sure I speak for the entire SMU community when I say I am delighted that he has joined our English Department."

The man being so honored was Robert Gilson formerly of University College, Oxford. He had come to SMU after his marriage plans fell apart and now taught a wildly popular course on the English Romantic Poets in Dallas Hall. Mr. Cody had read all of Gilson's novels and poetry and the two had corresponded over the years. When the job offer from SMU came up last summer, Mr. Cody had quickly offered Mr. Gilson his spacious guesthouse. Mr. Gilson was a young man and quite handsome and Francine Fisher, proprietor of the children's bookshop in Snider Plaza could not take her eyes off him. She saw in him the handsomeness of Shelley, the dangerousness of Bryon and the shyness of Keats. Unaware that she was speaking out loud she said, "He is absolutely perfect in every way."

The three men turned to the blushing woman and Mr. Cody said, "Why, Francine! What would your husband say?" Francine tried to pull herself together and replied, "Who? Oh, him. Well, never mind about him. He is home enjoying football and cartoons so I don't feel the least bit guilty about being here enjoying…. Oh my, perhaps we should get down to the business at hand."

It was delightful to see how the color rose in the flustered woman's cheeks but more teasing would have been cruel. "In that case, I can tell you all that the children responded excitedly to our little contest," Mr. Cody said.

"Wonderful," said Mr. Gilson. "I suppose now all we have to do is wait for their work to be submitted."

"That's right. So, if it meets with everyone's schedule, let's plan on meeting back here two weeks from now. My cook will keep us well fortified for what may be a very long day. Now, is it too early to toast ourselves with a little sherry?"

Both Professor Sylvest and Mr. Gilson agreed it was a splendid idea and Francine, who was at that moment listening to Mr. Gilson read some of his love sonnets to her on a beach in Mallorca, roused herself and said, "Oh, by all means! Pour away, pour away!"

When Thomas got home the fireplace in the den spread a welcoming warmth thanks to the good, split and aged logs Mr. Walton delivered right after Halloween. The table was set for lunch and his thawing nose told him that tomato soup and grilled cheese sandwiches would soon be defrosting his insides. His grandmother asked, "How was story hour?"

"It was fun. A good story about a family in Santa Fe. But the best part is there is a writing contest."

"Splendid," said his mother. "You are going to enter, aren't you? Your teacher brags to me about your book reports."

"I might, but this is different from book reports; in those I just have to write about something someone else has already written, now I have to create something out of thin air."

"Well, I have great confidence in you, son of mine. You can do anything you set your mind and heart to."

"Thanks, mom. I'll give it a try."

The lunch things were cleared away and plans for the rest of the day were discussed. Grandmother said, "Well, I think, considering the weather, it is the perfect day to stay indoors and do some baking. What do you think, Mae?"

"That sounds fine to me, Mama. The pantry has everything we need to make the Christmas breads for our neighbors."

"How about you, Carl? Anything you still need to tend to?"

"Oh, you know me, Clara. I enjoy this week more than any other the year has to offer. All the baking and decorating and especially the secret shopping! Think I will get out and see if I can find something for my special sweetheart. Who knows, I may just find something for you too!"

It was an old joke that was repeated throughout the year, Clara's birthday, St. Valentine's Day, their wedding anniversary, and Clara played her part in the fun by pretending to be angry with the old goof but always giving him a kiss. This time was no different and as she helped him into his overcoat she embraced her husband tightly and gave him a quick peck on the cheek.

"You be careful. You know these holiday drivers are thinking about everything but safety."

"Oh, I will be. I'll come home safe and sound and all in one piece. Wouldn't want you to have to go to all the great trouble of replacing me!"

"That may not be as hard as you imagine, Carl Matkin."

"Is that so? Well just where do you think you will find anyone who could possibly be as warm and witty and wonderful as yours truly."

"You are right, Carl. You are irreplaceable. Now go on and hurry back."

Clara and her daughter watched as Carl walked past the kitchen window on his way to the garage. "Yes, he would be hard to replace, Mama."

"Oh, you bet he would be. Why I would have to drive clear out to the lunatic asylum way out in East Texas to find anyone remotely like him!"

"Mama, that's an awful thing to say!" Mae was shocked.

"You know I am teasing, honey. No, he is truly a fine man in every way. My years with him have been joyous."

"Mama, you are very lucky to have him. I think he is the last good man on the face of the earth."

Clara and Carl were beginning to be concerned about their daughter. Sure, there were allowances to be made for a woman who had been through such an awful marriage but a lot of time had passed since she gathered the courage to leave Amarillo and all that horror. In a few weeks it would be 1962, six years after Mae arrived at their door. They were happy that she loved her teaching job and got on well with her colleagues but they were dismayed that she kept apart and did not participate in any events that were not school related, and she would attend those only if it was required. If she had any male admirers at all, Clara and Carl were unaware of them. Oh, Mae seemed happy enough and the Matkin household was certainly joyous with her and her son there, but parents can tell when something is amiss with one of their children. As much as they would hate to see her go, Clara and Carl hoped that someday Mae would begin her own life apart from them before her loneliness and sadness made her bitter and resentful and eventually resigned to live out her days alone in the big house on East Mockingbird Lane. Something needed to happen with

Mae. But what?

"You will find that there is at least one more good one out there somewhere who will make you every bit as happy as your father has made me. And when you do you will feel the rightness of it clear down to the soles of your feet!"

She hugged her daughter close and Mae said, "I hope you're right, mama. It may sound silly but even with you and daddy and Thomas to love, I have been rather…Oh, gracious. I am just being selfish."

"No, no you're not, honey. You're being human."

In the meantime, Thomas was sitting at his desk staring at a piece of blank paper. He kept tapping his forehead with his pencil hoping that action might make an idea appear. Ordinarily he would be out shopping with his grandfather at all their favorite places: Hillside Village, Casa Linda Plaza, maybe stop in to fill up the Buick at Raymond Truelove's and get some lunch at Roscoe White's BBQ, but he had to get busy if he really wanted to produce something for the contest. But now he was not so sure; he had no idea how hard it would be. He sat there at his desk staring out the window for a long time, the blank paper waiting patiently to be filled. "Oh, this is crazy! I'm going for a walk. Maybe I will see something to write about."

He bundled up and called from the front door, "I'm going up to Hillside Village. I'll be back later."

"Okay, honey," his mom said from the kitchen. "Don't forget to wear your gloves."

Good advice; it was really cold and blustery. Thomas made his way west on Mockingbird, crossed over the bridge, stopped for a minute to peek over the wall to look at the people stringing lights around the pond on Lange Circle, and finally made it to the shopping center. He stopped in the bakery first for two reasons: one, it would take some of the chill off his cheeks, and two, the girl behind the counter sometimes treated him to a cookie. He was not disappointed; sixteen-year-old Charlotte handed him a fresh from the oven oatmeal, pecan, and chocolate chip marvel wrapped in waxed paper. "Merry Christmas, Thomas," she said with a smile. Thomas thanked her but felt himself blushing; he thought he might have a "crush" on the pretty high school girl, but he was not even sure what a "crush" was. Next, he went into JoJo's Toys to have a look; he wished Willy a Merry Christmas at the barbershop, wandered around John Cobb's Drugstore, and then stopped in to visit Mr. Aldridge at the Book Nook.

"Well Thomas, what brings you out on this cold day?"

"I'm looking for ideas, Mr. Aldridge. Ideas for a story."

"Oh, the library's contest. I heard about that. Well, any luck?"

"Not yet."

Thomas looked around at all the shelves filled with books and asked, "Where did they come from, Mr. Aldridge? Where did the ideas for all these books come from?"

Mr. Aldridge relit his pipe and joined Thomas in the fiction section of the store. "For the most part they came from inside the writer, Thomas. Let me show you some examples. Look here; Charles Dickens. Well, he experienced a rough childhood so we have *Oliver Twist* and *Great Expectations* and so forth. Here's Ernest Hemingway; he knew first-hand about war and bullfights and hunting. There're *A Farewell to Arms*, *The Sun Also Rises*, a whole shelf of titles by him. And look here, Truman Capote who spent a lot of his childhood in the deep south and was cared for by a sweet old aunt and I know you know his books: *A Christmas Memory*, *The Thanksgiving Visitor*, and *One Christmas*."

"So, it looks like writers write about things that have happened to them, right."

"Yes and no, Thomas. Anyone can write about what they have experienced but the best writers have something that makes their experiences a part of your own. You can smell the ocean in Melville, you can hear the jazz in Fitzgerald, and you can feel the cold in Jack London. But for starts I think you should do what Hemingway told new writers: 'Write what you know.'"

Thomas thanked Mr. Aldridge and headed back home. And as he walked down Mockingbird Lane he wondered what it was he did know. "Well, let's see," he thought to himself. "What do I know? What has happened to me at Christmas that would make a good story? I could write about the time Robert Frost sent me that book or the time Captain Forrester's Christmas tree caught fire or the time Mr. Cody gave me my bicycle." Suddenly Thomas had more ideas than he needed. Which to choose? But by the time he got home and sat down at his desk, he knew. "I'll write about how I got here; about what Miss Johnson taught me about grownups, and about how my mom finally came here from Amarillo that Christmas Eve. That's it." And he wrote at the top of his paper:

"What Miss Johnson Taught."

ॐ

The day arrived! The contest winners were soon to be announced and the festively decorated Lakewood Library was full of aspiring authors and their families. Miss Johnson called for everyone's attention. "Now the moment is at hand. I want to thank all of you for coming but that is all I am going to say because I can't wait another minute to hear who won and I know you feel the same. So, Mr. Cody, if you would be so kind." Mr. Cody walked to the lectern. "I would like my fellow judges to join me here. Professor Sylvest, Mr. Gilson, Francine Fisher." As the three made their way through the crowd, Mr. Cody continued, "Let's show these fine people our appreciation for their commitment to this contest." Thunderous applause made it difficult for Clara to hear what Mae was saying to her but she gathered that her daughter was quite taken with the dashing Mr. Gilson. The applause died down and Mr. Cody continued, "I know I speak for all the judges when I say that it was extremely difficult to choose the winning stories. We are encouraged by the quality of writing each of you exhibited; it is clear that your language arts teachers are doing their jobs exceptionally well. But without further ado, (he covered the microphone and whispered to Mr. Gilson, I've always wanted to say that) here we go. We award third prize to entry number eleven, "The Princess Ballerina's Christmas in Paris." Diane squealed, "That's me, that's me!" And she pushed her way to collect her envelope from Mrs. Fisher.

"Second prize goes to number twenty-three, "Santa Claus Defeats the Moon Men." "Hey, that's you," Thomas said to his pal. "Go on up, go on up." Jon had been so busy making faces and gagging noises at Diane that he had not heard. "What? I won?" "Yes, now go get your prize!" Thomas gave him a good shove that propelled him to the front of the room. Jon was very happy to get the prize but perhaps his greatest pleasure came from seeing the complete and utter astonishment on Diane's face!

"And now for first prize. This story moved all of us deeply and we are sure it will move you too when you read it in this afternoon's paper. Number forty-eight, "What Miss Johnson Taught." Thomas couldn't move. It was one thing to write such a personal story, it was quite another to admit being the author.

"Oh, I do hope the winner is here with us this morning," said Mr. Cody. "Number forty-eight, are you here?"

Something stronger than his fear made Thomas reach into his pocket, raise the piece of paper with number forty-eight printed on it and say, "Yes, I'm here. I'm number forty-eight!" He made his way to the podium and received his envelope, and then he turned to receive the applause of those gathered. He saw his mother's bright smile and bright, tear-filled eyes.

The crowd moved into another part of the library where there were punch and Christmas cookies. Thomas was the center of attention, receiving congratulations from his classmates, and, as he stood with his family, Mr. Gilson approached him and introduced himself. Thomas said, "This is my grandmother and grandfather, Mr. Gilson. And this is my mother."

"Carl and Clara Matkin," said Grandfather taking Mr. Gilson's outstretched hand. "And this is our daughter, Mae Godwin."

"You should be very proud of this young man. He is quite a writer."

"Oh, we are," said Mae. "We are anxious to finally get to read his story. He has kept it a secret."

"I can safely say that you will enjoy it very much. Mr. Cody was right; we were all deeply moved. Congratulations, Thomas. Keep up the good work. I hope to see all of you again soon."

Mae, who had been trying to identify Mr. Gilson's cologne, said a little too loudly, "Oh, but you will! You are coming to our Christmas party tonight, aren't you?"

"Yes, that's right. Mr. Cody told me about your party. I wouldn't miss it for the world. May I come?"

Mae almost laughed out loud but controlled herself. "My family and I would be delighted to have you."

❧

Thomas was very nervous when the afternoon paper arrived and each member of his family passed his story from one to the other. Grandmother was crying as she passed it to Grandfather who, very unlike himself, hugged Thomas tightly as he passed it to Mae. She took it to her room and was in there with it a long time before she emerged with tears unsuccessfully wiped away from her cheeks.

"Oh, Thomas. This is beautiful," she said.

"You're not mad at me?"

"Why on earth should I be?"

"Well, I put in an awful lot of stuff in there about you, personal stuff about you and dad and the bad stuff and coming here and so on. I should have asked you first."

"No, you shouldn't have, Thomas. I want everyone to know how much my son cared about me when I was…well when things were so sad. Come here, son of mine, and let me give you a hug!"

࿇

As you might imagine, Thomas's story was the talk of the Christmas party at the big house on East Mockingbird Lane. Diane and Donna were quick to tell him that Christmas stories were supposed to be happy and that his was not happy at all! Jon wasn't sure what to say but he did hint that Thomas's story would have been better if he had put some Martians in it. Thomas was glad to sneak away with a plate of food to his room and watch Dale Milford on Channel 8 track Santa's flight on the weather radar. The rest of the house was filled with the regular attendees and their culinary specialties. Mr. Cody, who had arranged with Marcel's to have a case of Champagne and a case of sherry delivered to the Matkin's house earlier, arrived with Mr. Gilson who carried a blazing plum pudding. Mae, who was wearing a beautiful dark green velvet dress (the assembled guests agreed that she had never look lovelier) rushed forward, "Here let me take that. You're about to set your scarf on fire!"

"Thank you. Mr. Cody insisted we light it on the front porch. The man does love drama!" He followed her to the sideboard where she found a spot for the rich, dark cake.

"Yes," she agreed, "his entrances are legendary here in Lakewood. Follow me, I'll show you where you can leave your coat. I am so glad you came."

As they stood in the dark of the guest bedroom among the piles of coats, scarves and hats, Mr. Gilson said, "There is nowhere else on earth I would rather be. After reading your son's story I feel you and I have a lot in common; I think we have dealt with similar personal horrors and perhaps harbor some of the same fears as a result. Perhaps it would be beneficial to both of us to explore that possibility."

Their eyes locked and Mae did not know if an hour or a minute passed before she said, "Perhaps you're right. This is, after all, the season when anything is possible." They touched hands and Mae, her face as red as a holly berry, excused herself and rushed back to the dining room.

"Mama! You remember what you said about something feeling so right that I would feel it clear down to the soles of my feet? Well, this goes clear past the bottoms of my shoes, through the floor, through the foundation of the house, and clear to the center of the earth!"

THE LITTLE VISITOR

Carl Matkin operated what he liked to call "The Early Bird Diner." What it was, in fact, was a collection of bird feeders hung from the trees in the backyard of the big house on East Mockingbird Lane. While his wife was cooking breakfast this cold December morning, Carl took a peek through the bedroom curtains to see if he had any customers.

"Well, for Pete's sake! Clara, come in here!"

"What is it, Carl? Why all the shouting? Where are you?"

"I'm in our bedroom! Just come here and look at this!"

Clara, followed closely by her grandson, Thomas, left her breakfast preparations and hurried down the hallway.

"Oh, I bet he has spotted some bird and thinks the whole wide world should come to a stop," Clara said under her breath. "Some cardinal or starling or something. He just better not complain if his breakfast is cold, that's all I've got to say!"

"Grandfather sure likes his birds, doesn't he Grandmother?"

Sure enough, there was Carl Matkin holding his binoculars to his eyes and peeking at something through the barely parted curtains that opened onto the backyard.

"Just as I thought. What is it this time? A yellow-bellied sapsucker?"

"No, no, no. Nothing like that. Just come over here and take a look."

Grandmother went to the window and said, "Gracious, Carl. It is just a little boy!"

"I know it's just a little boy! But what in the Sam Hill is he doing in our backyard in the freezing cold?"

Thomas had made a space for himself at the window and said, "Looks like he is gathering up pecans and putting them in a lunch sack."

"Well I know that! But why?"

"No need to shout at Thomas, Carl. You asked what the boy was doing, not why he was doing it."

Thomas's mother, Mae, was drawn to the commotion and squeezed in between her mother and father. The glass was fogging up with their collective breath and she wiped away a clear circle with the cuff of her robe. She thought she recognized the boy but he was so bundled up that she couldn't be sure. Her schoolteacher's ability to identify individual students, even at great distances, was no help to her when it came to putting a name to this young man – she was not even certain it was a young man!

"Do you have any idea why that boy is out there?" her father asked.

"Nope, but there is one sure way to find out."

But by the time Mae had emerged into the backyard protected against the bitter wind by her winter coat and headscarf, the visitor was nowhere to be seen. Back in the house she said, "Well, that will just have to remain a mystery. Oh, my, it is cold out there!" She put her coat and scarf on one of the hooks by the door, poured a cup of coffee and helped her mother finish preparing breakfast.

Breakfast was Thomas's favorite meal of the day; no other meal in the Matkin home allowed so much indulgence: sausage, pancakes, butter, syrup, orange juice, biscuits, gravy, scrambled eggs. And not a sign of spinach, carrots, lima beans or Brussels sprouts anywhere! He was all set to dig in to his steaming plate when the doorbell sounded. Grandfather grumbled his way to the front door where, upon opening it, he stared down into a pair of blue eyes peeking out from between a thick wool scarf and cap. In fact, the little visitor was so completely wrapped up in wool garments that for a moment Grandfather thought maybe it was a large dog or maybe even a bear cub! A voice tried to make it ways through the scarf but it was no use. Grandfather said, "You'll have to speak up. I can't understand a word you're saying." But as difficult as it was for a voice to come out of that bundle of warmth it was equally hard for a voice to get in. The two stood there at an impasse, their muted dialogue getting them nowhere, until Grandmother solved the problem by inviting the visitor to come inside and remove some layers.

What emerged was a little boy about the age of six or seven who said in a practiced voice, "Good morning. I am selling fresh-picked, delicious Texas pecans. Would you like to buy some?" He then reached deep inside his big coat and extracted a bulging lunch sack. "They are only twenty-five cents a bag and I fill it almost all the way to the top. See?"

Grandfather and Grandmother looked at each other in amused befuddlement and for a rare moment Grandfather found himself speechless in the face of such a bold enterprise. He was all set to explain to the hopeful boy the absurdity of asking a man to buy back his own pecans even if they were only twenty-five cents and the bag overflowing! But Grandmother knew what was coming and cut him off, "Well of course we will buy some. How many bags do you have?" "I just have four right now but I can come back with more later." "I'll just bet you can," muttered Grandfather but a look from Grandmother put an end to any further speculations on his part. "Carl, give the young man a dollar." Pecans and money equitably exchanged, the boy began the process of bundling up again. Mae, who had been looking closely at the boy said, "Oh, I think I recognize you now. You're Tim Miller, aren't you? In Miss Savard's first grade class?"

"Yes, ma'am. That's me."

"Well, don't run off. Can you sit and have some breakfast with us? You know who I am, don't you?"

"Yes, ma'am. You're Miss Godwin. You teach the big kids."

"That's right. And do you know my son Thomas."

"Sure. He was my best customer when I had that Kool-Aid stand last summer."

The two "men" shook hands. "Yeah," Thomas said, "I sure looked forward to that cup of Kool-Aid after throwing my papers. Last summer was a hot one!"

Mae said, "Come have something before you go back out into that cold wind. Have you had your breakfast? Would you like some hot chocolate?"

Soon Tim was thawing his nose over the steam rising from his big mug of chocolate and little marshmallows. He emptied the mug and wiped the foamy brown mustache off his upper lip and made his thank yous and good-byes.

"I've gotta get back to selling. Christmas is next week and I need to make some more money," he said as he climbed into his coat.

"Got a lot of presents to buy, have you?" asked Grandfather.

"Just a few. But I want to give my dad something big this year. He's been real sick."

"Oh, I'm sorry." Grandmother said as she settled his hat in place. "What's wrong with him?"

"He's had a real bad cold for a while and it got so bad that he had to go into the hospital. That's where he is now. Mama says I'm the man of the house now. But when he comes home I want to cheer him up with a present I know he wants."

"And what might that be?" Grandmother asked.

"Well, the other day before he went to the hospital I heard him and mama talking and he said this Christmas he wants a motorcycle or a set of golf clubs. They laughed so hard about that they both had tears in their eyes when I came in the room. So I need to get going. I've made eleven dollars so I'm guessing the motorcycle is out. But eleven dollars should be enough for a swell set of golf clubs, don't you think?"

It took everything Mae had to not burst into tears before the door closed on the early morning visitor, but once he was out of hearing she let loose with deep sobs and hurried to the kitchen. When she returned to the dining room she explained to her astonished family that she knew more about Tim's situation and it just broke her heart.

"There are a few of us at school who know that Tim's father has prostate cancer. Miss Savard keeps in touch with Mrs. Miller and reports the latest news to us in private. From what I've heard he had his surgery yesterday and his doctor said that since Mr. Miller was smart enough to get an annual checkup they managed to catch it in its early stages and there is every reason to think they removed all of it. But only time and tests can tell for sure so they are keeping him in the hospital for no one knows how long. She told me the entire family is riding a fast roller coaster of emotions and no one knows what to tell Tim. They all finally agreed that maybe it would be best to spare him any grief by telling him his father has a very bad cold and the doctors want to keep him with them for a while."

"What about his mother," Grandfather asked. "How is she coping?"

"As well as can be expected, I suppose. Miss Savard said that Tim's grandparent's, his father's mom and dad, have moved in and are giving Mrs. Miller all the help they can. But the big question is what to do about Tim now that school's out for Christmas."

"It's hard to know what to tell a child in a situation like this. I suppose it depends on the child but I'll be darned if I know what I would do in their shoes. I take it the boy and his daddy are very close," said Grandfather.

"Oh, they are. And this is their favorite time of year. Mr. Miller goes all out at Christmas, pretty much like we do. Now, with his father in the hospital and his mother and grandparents going back and forth, Tim has been kind of left to fend for himself. I could tell this morning that he is confused and starting to get scared."

"Yes, he is a sharp boy." Grandfather said. "You know he is working hard to convince himself that the 'has a bad cold' story is true."

Grandmother, who had been quiet a lot longer than usual, burst in, "Well, there is just one thing to do! Tim will spend these days with us! I will call his house and make the offer. Everyone all right with that idea? Thomas?"

Thomas hesitated.

"Now Thomas," his mother said, "surely you can entertain Tim for a few days, can't you? After all, your best friend Jon is in Corpus Christi visiting family. It seems to me you would like to have someone your age to share Christmas activities with."

But that was just it; Tim was not Thomas's age. And while a few years difference doesn't matter so much later in life, to Thomas it was a gap as wide as the Grand Canyon.

"Well, I guess I could. He's awfully young, though."

Mae laughed and put her arms around him. "That's my boy!"

"Then it is all settled. Right, Carl?"

"Sure, sure. Go ahead and call their house. Tell them Thomas and I will drive over and pick Tim up when they are ready."

Grandmother and Mae sprang to action and Thomas and Grandfather stood wondering what they had gotten themselves into, as usual.

~

After breakfast the next morning, Grandfather guided the Buick out of the driveway and onto East Mockingbird Lane. The sky was steely cold and the light raindrops looked like they could become snowflakes if they just tried a little harder. The driver and his passenger could see their breath fog the windshield until the car's defroster wiped it clean. As they neared Tim's house Grandfather said, "Okay, here is how it is going to be, as well as I can understand your mother and grandmother. Tim's family is happy to have him spend the days with us but we need to bring him home each evening and on no account are we to tell him what we know about how truly ill his father is. Okay Thomas? Thomas? You seem distracted, boy."

"Oh, sorry, Grandfather. Sure, I can keep quiet about his dad. I was just thinking how strange it is that something bad can happen at Christmastime. Seems to me that it should be a time when you are protected somehow and nothing can hurt you or make you cry."

"You remember don't you, it was not too long ago that you dropped more than a few tears on Christmas."

"Yes, sir. That was when I first came to live with you and Grandmother and I was worried about my mom."

"You've experienced a few magical Christmases since that hard time, haven't you?"

"I sure have. It's hard to think though, especially this time of year when our family is very happy, that some families are very sad."

"Unfortunately, there are lots of folks who are, for one reason or another, and we must do our best to help them if we can. Especially this time of year when we are lucky enough to be so very happy, as you said."

"I'll remember that, Grandfather."

The Buick had just crossed the dividing line between the street and the Miller's driveway when Tim shot out the front door of his house and climbed into the back seat. Three adults waved from the front door and Carl returned their greeting.

"That's my mama, my grandma and my grandpa. They told me to tell you thanks again, Mr. Matkin."

"We are happy to have you join us, Tim. Aren't we Thomas?"

"You bet. We do a lot of fun things at our house for Christmas. And it looks like a bad day for selling pecans."

"Well," Tim confessed, "That business is over. I tried to sell some to Mrs. Petteway and she called my mama and got real mad. So, my mama said I'd better quit it. But that's all right; I've got eleven dollars to spend and that's plenty."

"Your house looks all set, Tim. I see you have your Christmas tree there in the front window, and lights around your roof," said Carl.

"My grandpa has been doing all the things my daddy usually does. I help some and we have a good time but when he doesn't know I'm looking at him he looks sad."

When they got inside the big house on East Mockingbird they all agreed it was just too cold and wet to do anything other than take care of all the indoor work that needed to be done. Tim was not shy about pitching in: he helped Mae and Clara with the baking, the wrapping, the decorating…then he would sit still long enough to add a few pieces to the jigsaw puzzle Grandfather and Thomas had started. There was a big lunch of grilled cheese sandwiches and tomato soup and Tim helped clear the table, dry the dishes and put them away. After all that activity, it did not take the warm fire and the deep cozy chair in the den long to send Tim into a deep, peaceful nap.

This routine was repeated the next day but the day after that was set aside for last minute shopping. For once they all went out together, agreeing to separate in the shops they visited and solemnly promising not to try and sneak a peek at what anyone was buying. It must be kept secret! The big Sear Roebuck on Ross Avenue was the first stop, but before going in the boys wanted to see the Santa's Workshop display in the corner window. And there it was! So much to take in! Animated elves everywhere, busy making toys; Santa in his huge armchair going over his long list of good little boys and girls.

"There's my name!" Tim shouted. "And yours too, Thomas!"

Clara leaned in close to her husband and whispered, "I don't see "Carl" on that list, my dear."

"Oh, well, Santa knows I don't like to have a big fuss made of how good I've been all year." He hugged his wife tight and added, "I'm not worried. He has never failed me yet!"

A quick kiss and they hurried the boys and Mae into the store. Oh, the store! So beautifully decorated and filled with the sounds of Christmas. And the aromas from the candy counter! Mae and Grandmother went one direction and Grandfather led the boys toward the sporting goods. Grandfather knew Tim was in for a disappointment when the boy discovered that a set of golf clubs was far beyond his budget but he was ready with an alternative suggestion that just might do the trick. Sure enough Tim spotted a bright red bag filled with shiny clubs, looked at the sales tag and was crestfallen.

"Why, I don't think eleven dollars will buy even one of these clubs."

The light was going out of his bright eyes, but Grandfather was quick!

"Tell me something, Tim. What kind of clubs does your dad have now?"

"Oh, he doesn't have any at all. He's just kind of hinted he would like to start playing someday."

Grandfather bent down on cracking knees to look the boy in the face and said, "One thing about golf clubs is that they have to fit the golfer. They must be just the right length, weight, grip, all sorts of things. So, it is best for first-time golfers to choose the right set themselves. But what all first-time golfers need and are pretty much the same for everyone are golf balls and tees. Look here, here is a box of the kind of balls I like and here is a little box of tees. Any golfer would love to get these for Christmas, Tim, and they won't break your bank."

The boy brightened and hugged the good old man, nearly sending them both head over heels into a display of camping gear!

After a while, purchases safely stored in the Buick's deep trunk, the happy group made their way to other stops: Jojo's toys (Thomas and Tim had to wait an agonizingly long time in the car) John Cobb's, The Book Nook, and even as cold as it was that day, they did not hesitate or think twice about going out of their way to wish Merry Christmas to Willy at the barber shop or Charlotte at the bakery and so many others. Because he had been so patient with them and their demands (changing directions, going back to shops they had already been to twice!) Mae and Grandmother let Grandfather choose where to have lunch and in an instant they were comfortably seated in Grandfather's favorite place, Roscoe White's BBQ. Happily filled, and after a stop at Raymond Truelove's to gas up the Buick and wish Raymond and Little Ray a Merry Christmas, the group settled into a long afternoon of wrapping, baking, puzzle building, storytelling and all the other pleasant pastimes of the season.

Christmas Eve! Here it was at last! Preparations for the Matkin's party that night were in full swing. Furniture dusted, candles replaced, just a few more ornaments added to an enormous Fraser fir that was so over-laden already that it was a testament to the solid construction of the living room floor, and, (can it be believed?), here is a present thought to have already been wrapped hiding in the back of the hall closet! Quick, get out the wrapping paper and ribbons again! Grandfather, Thomas and Tim had been assigned the enviable chore of filling the gumdrop trees with sugary red and green gumdrops. It was noticed by all that Tim, who had been so active and excited all the previous days he had spent with them, was slowing down in his enthusiasms and becoming very quiet and withdrawn. In fact, when he finished his tree, he asked if it would be all right if he went to lie down for a while.

Thomas, who liked the younger boy despite being so much more "grown up," was astonished. "Lie down on Christmas Eve?" he sputtered, "Why, I don't think I could ever..." But his mother's eyes cautioned him.

"Aren't you feeling well, Tim? Did more of those gum drops go into you than onto your tree?" Mae asked.

"No, it's not that. I'm just a little tired, that's all. I really kind of want to go home."

"But Tim, there is no one there right now. They are all at the hospital with your dad. But your grandparents will be here after a little while for tonight's party."

The boy started to cry and Mae gently guided him back to Thomas's room. "Now, now, Tim. You just go ahead and have a good cry," Mae said as she settled him on the twin bed. "I'll just sit here beside you if you find you want to talk about anything."

"I'm sorry," the boy sniffed, "it's just that I miss my dad so much. I don't know why he is not home and I don't know why I can't go see him. I'm having a swell time with you all but it's just not... Oh, I don't know! There are things I need to be doing with my dad, things we always do together, things he needs my help to do right!"

It tore at Mae's heart that there was really nothing she could do or say to take away the hurt so she just stroked the little boy's hair as he sobbed into the pillow and eventually fell into merciful sleep.

Later that evening, the big house on East Mockingbird was filled with all the happiness the mysteries of Christmas Eve bring every year. Rooms were filled with people, food, laughter and music. Thomas was in his element, answering the door and helping with the additions to the feast each guest brought. The Lueckes, Miss

Bradford, the Clines were there, and so were Mrs. Petteway, and dear Mr. Cody and his houseguest Mr. Gilson with their plum pudding and sherry and Champagne (Mr. Gilson, in addition to being on loan from Oxford University to SMU, was courting Mae, much to the dismay of all eligible and even some ineligible women in the Lakewood community!). Oh, all the comfort that never varying traditions can bring! There was one couple, however, Thomas opened the door to that he did not recognize but it seemed he had seen them somewhere.

"Merry Christmas," the man said, "You must be Thomas. We are Tim's grandparents."

"Now I remember," said Thomas, "come in. Merry Christmas to you, too."

"Thank you. Where's our Timmy?" Tim's grandmother asked as she tried to find him among all the guests.

"Well, uh, he's uh..." Thomas didn't know what to say and he was relieved when his mother came to his rescue.

"Hello, I'm Mae Godwin. I'll take you to Tim. He's down the hallway in Thomas's room. But first..." Mae told the grandparents about Tim's sadness and how they had been unable to coax the boy to join the party; how he said he just wanted to be alone.

"Oh, my poor Timmy," said Tim's grandmother.

Clara and Carl joined Mae. "Welcome, folks. How is your son?" Carl asked.

"Exhausted, scared, determined, hopeful. Optimistic one minute, pessimistic the next," Tim's grandfather answered. "Sure has missed his Tim. We had hoped he could come home for Christmas...." his voice caught for a second but then continued, "Our boy has a great doctor and he thinks he got the cancer out of all the surrounding area but they need to run some more tests."

"And his nurse, dear, don't forget his nurse," Tim's grandmother added.

"Oh, she is really something. Came here straight from school at Yale where she learned of something called the Hospice Movement that has started over in England. Claims it will revolutionize patient care in this country, if she has anything to say about it. Very determined. She has been fighting like a wildcat to get the doctor to let our boy come home for a few days. Said she would camp out at our house and take care of him herself if it came to that."

Mrs. Petteway interrupted, "Clara, your phone has been ringing off the hook so I finally answered it. Someone is asking to speak to a Mr. or Mrs. Miller."

"I bet that's our daughter. We told her to call here if there was any news."

"I'll show you to the phone, its right this way." Clara led the Millers to the den and it wasn't long before Mr. Miller hung up and let out a joyous "Whoop!"

"That blessed nurse won the day! Our boy is on his way home right now. Just for a few days, he has to go back for some tests, but that wonderful, wonderful nurse shook the latest test results under the doctor's nose and convinced him to release our boy this very night!"

Even though most of the people in the house had no idea what was going on, they all burst into cheers and applause, so contagious was the Miller's joy. What good news! Mrs. Miller was driving Mr. Miller home for Christmas! Why, they are probably there now!

Little Tim, awakened by the uproar, came sleepily into the room rubbing his eyes. His grandmother quickly grabbed him up into her arms and said, "Time to go, Tim, time to go! There is someone waiting at home who is anxious to see you!"

"Santa?" the drowsy boy asked.

"Even better than Santa, Timmy! Even better!".

A PEACOCK IN A PECAN TREE

The day before Thanksgiving was the busiest of the year for the Casa Linda Bakery. Every shelf and surface was covered with white pastry boxes waiting to be picked up by customers who would stream in and out of the shop from the moment the sign in the door was turned from "Closed" to "Open" and, finally, back to "Closed" again. Mrs. Mason and her staff, three high school girls who worked for her on Saturdays and school holidays, had all in readiness when the first car pulled up to the curb at 8:00 a.m.

"Here we go, girls! Penny, would you turn the sign and unlock the door please?"

"Yes, ma'am."

Mrs. Mason had seen many girls come and go during the years she had owned the shop. Some came back to report on how their lives had progressed; some were never seen or heard from again. That didn't matter though; her heart was large enough to hold all "her girls" and she liked to think she had had some positive influence on each one. Penny, however, puzzled her. Oh, she had no complaints about the girl; Penny was always well groomed, polite with the customers, quick to learn, and could always find something that needed to be done in the shop during slow times without prompting. She was very pretty, too; a tall, blue-eyed brunette sixteen-year-old whose smile lit up her face. What concerned Mrs. Mason was a sense of profound sadness that would sometimes show through Penny's eyes. Just for a moment Penny's shoulders might droop and her head bow and Mrs. Mason would ask, "Penny, dear, are you all right?" Penny would dab her eyes quickly and say, "Oh, I'm fine, really, Mrs. Mason", but Mrs. Mason was not so sure. Today, however, was not the day to dwell on it; customers were arriving and the little bell on the door was ringing vigorously!

❧

Thomas's grandmother was a wonderful cook in every way; but for some reason she had never gotten the hang of baking flaky piecrusts. It didn't take many failed attempts before she gave up and gladly turned to the talents of Mrs. Mason when an occasion called for pie. She went into the den where her grandson and husband were bent over a jigsaw puzzle. The border was all that had been fitted together of what was eventually going to reveal a lovely scene of winter in New England. All the other pieces were scattered over the card table they had set up by the fireplace.

"Would one of you be a gentleman and go pick up my order at the bakery, please?"

Thomas, who had just gotten his driver's license and looked for any opportunity to run an errand, was up and out of his chair like he had sat on a tack.

"I'll go, Grandmother! All right, Grandfather?"

"Sure, we can finish this later. I need a break anyway; my eyes are starting to cross."

"You go lie down and rest them, dear," Grandmother said. "Thomas can run this errand by himself."

"I keep forgetting he's all grown up and doesn't need his broken down old grandpa to drive him around anymore."

"I need you for plenty of other things, Grandfather, you know that."

Grandfather mussed Thomas's hair and said, "I know, I know. I was just teasing. Now you run along."

"I'll go ask Mom if there is anything she needs me to take care of while I'm out."

Thomas found his mother in the kitchen scooping out the yolks of hard-boiled eggs and putting them in a mixing bowl.

"Mom, would it be all right if I used your car to go to the bakery?"

"Sure, Thomas. I've got my hands full making the filling for tomorrow's deviled eggs. The keys are right there by the back door."

Thomas took the keys off the hook and asked, "Do you need me to get anything for you?"

"No, I do believe I have everything I need to prepare my part of the feast; but thanks."

"Do you think it would be okay if I took the long route to the bakery? You know how beautiful it is along Williamson Road this time of year. Just like a picture out of *Yankee Magazine*."

"Sure, you go ahead. Just be careful and keep your eyes on the road. There are some tricky parts."

Thomas knew that all too well. Two classmates of his had hit a tree hard at a particularly bad spot last year and died. The city had put up a couple of stop signs afterwards but most people felt the road could use more.

"I'll watch out, Mom."

Mae watched as her son ran to the car. She couldn't believe how tall and strong he had grown – seemingly overnight! It made her proud and sad at the same time because she knew he would soon be off to college and the lives of all those who lived in the big house on East Mockingbird would change quickly and forever.

෨

Thomas would remember it for the rest of his life: the moment he walked into the bakery and saw her behind the counter.

Of course, he had seen her before; she and her father had moved just across the street last summer. But, for some reason, this time was different. He felt something snap deep inside his chest that seemed to affect his ability to talk.

"Hi. You're Thomas, aren't you?" Penny said.

Thomas, amazed she knew who he was could only manage, "Uh."

"Are you here to pick up your Grandmother's order?"

"Uh," said Thomas.

"Well of course you are. Why else would you be here? Certainly not to visit me, right?"

"Uh," said Thomas.

"Here they are. Three pies: a pumpkin, a pecan and a chocolate. The chocolate must be for you, right?"

"Uh," said Thomas.

"That will be nine dollars and seventy-five cents."

Thomas somehow raised his arm and handed her a twenty-dollar bill. Penny put a ten and a quarter in his palm and held it there. She looked directly into his eyes and said, "Thank you, Thomas" so sweetly that Thomas felt every ounce of his blood rise to his face. He had to get out of there!

"Uh, I'm welcome. No, I mean, I'm sorry. No, YOU'RE welcome. What I mean is ... bye!" He pulled on the door a few times then realized the little sign above the handle read "Push." Finally, in the car, he took the first deep breath he had had in a long time and headed home.

In the bakery, Mrs. Mason watched Penny watch him leave. "Well," she thought, "there is nothing to worry about regarding this young lady. But that Thomas, oh dear, oh dear!" She suddenly laughed out loud and Penny turned to see what was so funny. When she saw what Mrs. Mason was pointing at on the counter, she laughed with her until both had tears running down their cheeks.

❧

Thomas arrived home feeling very full of himself. His mind had taken him through every emotional variation possible and he finally chose one and stuck with it. He was HAPPY! Over and over he said, "I think she likes me! Can you imagine that?"

"I'm home," he called from the kitchen.

"We're in the den, Thomas," said Grandmother. She sounded funny to him. He went into the den and saw Grandmother and his mom dabbing at their eyes. Grandfather had his back to him.

"Well, Thomas," said Grandfather, "Did you have a nice ride."

"I sure did. Williamson Road is every bit as pretty as the puzzle we are working on."

"Aren't you forgetting something."

"Oh, sure. Here's the change."

"Change from what, Thomas?"

"You know. From the money you gave me for the … Omigosh! I forgot the pies! I walked out and left them right there on the counter!"

The den exploded with laughter. Thoroughly embarrassed, Thomas said, "I'll go back and get them this minute. I am so sorry."

"No, no, Thomas," said Grandmother. "Mrs. Mason called and, when she could stop laughing long enough, told me what happened. She said Penny and her father would bring them over when they got home."

"Oh. Okay. I sure feel dumb."

"It's all right, Thomas. Come on, let's finish up this puzzle," said Grandfather.

His Mom and Grandmother went to the kitchen and Thomas and Grandfather took up their places and the card table.

"She's quite a looker, isn't she my boy?"

"Who?"

"Why that Penny McPherson, of course. I'll bet she's the only girl in the world who could make you forget pie!"

"Do you know her, Grandfather."

"No, but I have chatted a few times with her father, though. Nice fella. He's had a rough time."

"How's that, Grandfather?"

"Well, his wife, Penny's mother, died of breast cancer a couple of years ago. He was an English teacher up in Maine and he thought that moving away would make it easier to deal with his loss. But, a loved one does not live in just a particular geographic location, Thomas. Oh no. He soon found out that she lived in his heart no matter where he was. He doesn't regret the move though. He had read about the teacher shortage here in Dallas and he's really happy down at Stonewall Jackson. But the teacher pay here is so pitiful that he works on weekends at Adam's Paint Shop in Hillside Village. His daughter helps out by earning her own spending money at the bakery. She's real smart, too. The Episcopal School granted her a full scholarship."

"So, that's why I have never seen her at Woodrow."

"Ah ha! So, you do have eyes for her, don't you?"

"Gosh, Grandfather. I wouldn't know the first thing to say to her. You should have seen me at the bakery. She must think I am completely goofy."

"Would you like a little advice? I was once a pretty smooth operator."

Thomas had no trouble believing that. Even now, close to retirement, Carl Matkin possessed the dashing good looks that leading men had in old movies. Sort of a Fred Astaire with a Clark Gable mustache – no, more like William Powell in *The Thin Man*.

"I can certainly use all the help you would give me, Grandfather."

"First of all, find something she is interested in and you show some interest in it too. For instance, every afternoon she takes their Golden Retriever for a walk. Just happen to be out in the front yard when they are and say something nice about the dog, ask its name, that sort of thing. Before you know it, she may ask you to join them."

The doorbell rang and Thomas got up to answer it. He opened the door and there stood Penny holding three boxes.

"I wouldn't do this for just anybody, you know," she said.

"Thanks a lot. I'm sorry to cause you any trouble."

He looked so worried that she smiled and said, "It is no trouble at all, Thomas, really." They stood looking at each other for a while and Penny finally said, "Well, I need to get home and take our dog for an evening stroll."

"He sure is a good-looking dog. What's his name?"

"Her name is Snowball. Oh, I know, a big yellow dog named Snowball. Silly, huh? But she was as white and round as a snowball when we got her and that is the name we gave her. If you're not doing anything, why don't you join us?"

"Great! Let me get my jacket and I'll meet you at the sidewalk."

He turned to go and Penny said, "Thomas, the pies."

"Oh, yeah. Sorry." He took the three boxes and she said, "See you in a little bit."

As he passed through the den on his way to the kitchen, he said, "Grandfather, you are a genius!"

Grandfather called out to the blur that ran past him, "I am glad you have finally joined the rest of the world in recognizing that fact!"

∂ॐ

Penny and Thomas walked down a narrow lane toward White Rock Lake. She wore a navy pea jacket and matching beret and, even though it was freezing cold outside, she smelled like Mr. McShan's flower shop on a warm day. Snowball, excited by this stranger, did everything she could to get Thomas's attention. Penny and Thomas hardly knew she was there.

"What's the book in your jacket pocket?" Penny asked.

"Oh, it's *A Christmas Carol*. I read it every year. I start it around Thanksgiving and finish it on Christmas Eve. I carry it with me wherever I go."

"That's funny. I always carry a book with me too." She reached into an inside pocket in her pea jacket and produced *The Collected Poems of Emily Dickinson*. "She is my favorite. There's a bench down by the lake where I like to sit and read while Snowball explores. Let's go there."

They had not taken two steps when Penny shouted, "Thomas! Would you take a look at that!"

Thomas looked up and saw what had brought Penny to a halt. On a branch of an enormous pecan tree that rose behind a high brick wall, stood a peacock!

"Have you ever in your life seen anything so magnificent? It's beautiful! Look at that tail! Where we lived before, my mother had a tall vase filled with peacock tail feathers. I thought it was the most exotic thing in the entire world and I was going to get to have it in my room here in our new house. But the vase and all the feathers got lost in the move."

"Maybe we can get some for you from whoever lives here."

"Oh, wouldn't that be grand! But it is almost dark and I should be getting home. Dad and I are leaving early in the morning."

Penny and her father were going to visit his brother in Santa Fe for Thanksgiving and would not be back until Saturday night. They returned to their homes promising to meet on Sunday and make an attempt to get some feathers.

❧

Thanksgiving morning, however, Thomas was up before the rest of the house and on his way back to that high wall. He was determined to have a surprise for Penny when she got home. Soon he was at the spot where they had seen the peacock. He followed the wall around to where there stood a large, strongly locked, wrought iron gate. There was what he guessed was an intercom box mounted on the brick wall next to the gate and he pressed the button. There was no response. He tried holding the button down and saying, "Hello. Hello." Again, there was no response. Through the gate, he could see two figures in a big window at the front of the house.

"This thing must be broken," he thought.

He jumped up and down, waving his arms, hoping to attract their attention. They did not look in his direction.

"Well, I am just going to have to try something else."

He walked around to the spot where the pecan tree hung over the brick wall. The bricks were old and some were missing and that afforded Thomas a good hold; enough that with just a little effort he was soon sitting on top of the wall.

"Now, how do I get down?" he wondered.

He decided to work his way over to the pecan tree and by carefully climbing through its limbs reach a point where a leap to the ground would not result in any damage to him or the tree. He was doing just fine when he suddenly remembered that Grandfather had always referred to pecan trees as "self-pruners."

"Why would I think about a thing like that at a time like this?"

He took a step onto a particularly sturdy looking limb and there was a crack as loud as a rifle shot. The next thing he knew, he was on the ground, his right ankle bent in a way ankles were not meant to bend.

"What in the Sam Hill are you doing on my property?" shouted a tiny woman who was bearing down on him from the house, followed by a huge man. Thomas could not move. They soon stood above him.

"I'll ask you again: what are you doing on my property?" the woman demanded in a voice that was every bit as harsh as a blue jay's.

"I came to ask if you would do me a favor, ma'am," said Thomas who was just beginning to feel the pain in his ankle.

"A favor! From me? Why I ought to have you hauled off for trespassing? I ought to sue you for destroying my tree!"

The woman soon wore herself out and finally said, "Roberts, carry this boy into the house and call his family."

The giant said, "Yes, Madam" and lifted Thomas like he was nothing more than a bag of marshmallows.

"You do have a family, don't you boy?"

"Yes, ma'am. We live up the road on East Mockingbird."

He gave her his phone number and Roberts went to make the call after he had gently deposited Thomas onto a sofa in a large, dimly lit room.

The chair she sat in across from him dwarfed the woman. Thomas said, "I am sorry to cause you this trouble, ma'am. I just want to see if I could have some peacock tail feathers. I am able to pay for them. Despite appearances I really didn't come here to steal anything."

"Tail feathers? Why on earth do you want tail feathers?"

"Well, you see, there's this girl named Penny…"

"Stop right there! Do you mean to tell me you were up in my pecan tree risking your neck for some girl?"

"Yes, ma'am, I guess I was." And he told her Penny's story.

"What foolishness! I suppose you don't know any better. Kindness just leads to disappointment and giving your heart to another will cause you more pain than any human being should have to bear."

Thomas was in no mood to disagree. His ankle was throbbing and he was feeling light-headed. Fortunately, he was saved from further discussion by the arrival of Grandfather.

❧

For four weeks, Thomas hobbled around his home on crutches, his right foot in a cast that reached up nearly to his knee. Oh, he was treated like a Persian prince all right; but the old woman's words dampened his spirits. One afternoon, he told Grandmother what she had said.

"Oh, Thomas, you of all people know that's not true. Have you ever regretted any kindness you have shown to another? What about the letter you sent to your mother that gave her the courage to make the move that changed her life? Did Mr. Frost disappoint you when he heard about what happened to your mother's treasured book of his poems? But even if those things had not turned out so well, you would have known that you tried your best to do something good and you would have tried again."

"Why do you suppose that woman is so bitter and mean spirited? When Grandfather came to get me that morning she would not even talk to him. She just told Roberts to carry me to the car and turned her back. I realized that my book had fallen out of my jacket pocket when he lifted me but I couldn't bring myself to ask her for it. I just wanted to get far away from her and her gloomy house."

"I can tell you a little about her. You see, she and I went to high school together at Woodrow. Oh, we weren't close friends or anything; she was in the theatrical crowd and I had to give every minute I had to academics, but we were both over-achievers and we admired each other for that. Sylvia Groves; she had a beautiful voice and could act up a storm. I heard later that she had gone on to become quite famous in the world of opera and traveled to all sorts of exciting countries. But somewhere along the way someone broke her heart and she quit performing. She sold all her homes and gathered her most prized possessions into that house overlooking the lake. She shut herself up there surrounded by her memories. I suppose those peacocks she raises remind her of some place she once lived. Anyway, that's all I really know. She never leaves the grounds and you are the only person I know who has been inside her house, other than Roberts who has been with her forever."

"But Mom had her heart broken when Dad left us and she's not like that."

"Well, your mama had all of us to help her get back up after she had been knocked down. Most people just can't do it alone and I suspect that Miss Groves, although she had a lot of admirers, didn't have a friend in the world she could turn to. Now, I've got to get busy."

Grandmother left him there by the fire with his leg propped up. It was the worst time of the year for this to have happened to him. He didn't mind so much that the cast was cumbersome; he soon got used to hanging it over the bathtub when he bathed and he had rigged up an effective scratcher out of a wire coat hanger that fit easily down inside to ease some sudden torment. He wasn't worried about getting behind in school because his best friend Jon brought him his homework and returned the work Thomas had completed to his teachers. It was just hard for him to watch others doing things that had always been his responsibilities: bringing in the firewood, decorating the gaslight with the kit from the gas company that made it look like a candy cane, putting up the lights around the roof. Penny and her father were over almost every day. Mr. McPherson helped Grandfather bring in the tree and string the lights. Penny and Mom and Grandmother decorated and baked and shopped. Even though they encouraged Thomas to help, he felt clumsy and in the way.

Christmas Eve was difficult too. He decided he would not go to the Family Service at St. Matthew's. He told his family he would rather stay home than try to kneel and stand and sit (what he liked to call "Anglican gym class") over and over again. His mother understood and said, "All right for this year, mister. But we all will expect a great deal more involvement from you next Christmas!" That made him feel better as he watched them leave that night. Thomas fell asleep in the silence that is unique to Christmas Eve with the pleasantly unsettling feeling that a change was in the air.

❧

Christmas morning activities did not begin at the crack of dawn now that Thomas was sixteen, but the excitement, which was ageless, brought the family together in the hallway fairly early. No one could move until Grandfather had gone ahead into the living room to make sure Santa was not still there.

"Okay, he's been and gone. The glass of milk is empty and there's nothing but crumbs on the cookie plate!"

Thomas felt a little silly but he remembered his Grandmother telling him that Christmas is the one day of the year when everyone can be a child again. The floor around the Christmas tree was soon a mass of paper and ribbon and empty boxes. Once again they had broken their annual pledge that they would stick to a budget and not be so extravagant. After all the gasps of surprise and heart-felt thank yous, there was clean up and breakfast. Then work began for the Christmas dinner. This year, in addition to Mrs. Dodd and her daughters and Mrs. Petteway, Mr. McPherson and Penny were invited. Thomas was anxious to see Penny's reaction to the gift that his mother had found for him to give her: a silver bookmark with an etched portrait of Emily Dickinson and some lines of her poetry on it.

In the late afternoon, the guests began to arrive and were gathered around the punch bowl when Mrs. Dodd said, "Now who could this late arrival be?" Everyone turned to look through the dining room window at the ancient black car that had stopped in front of the house. Thomas stood frozen in place when he saw Roberts get out and open the door for ... could it be Miss Groves? It certainly resembled her in stature but this person had a smile on her face that positively radiated happiness! Grandfather was at the front door in an instant and led her and Roberts inside.

"Merry Christmas, all," said Miss Groves in a voice that almost sang with joy. "May I intrude for just a moment?"

"You're not intruding at all, Sylvia, you are welcome to join us," said Grandmother.

Miss Groves approached Grandmother and said, "Why Clara, it has certainly been a long time."

"Much too long, Sylvia. Can you join us for dinner?"

"I would like that very much, Clara, but first I have some business to take care of with your grandson."

She turned to Thomas, who fully expected to be handed a summons or subpoena or some sort of legal papers, and said, "I believe you left this on my lawn, young man," and handed him a book. It was *A Christmas Carol* all right but it was not Thomas's.

"This is not mine, Miss Groves. Mine was just an old paperback this one looks like real leather." He opened it and exclaimed, "Look at this; it has all the old original illustrations!"

"If you don't like it I could get you a newer one," Miss Groves teased.

"Oh no, Oh yes. I mean, this is incredible!"

"No, Thomas, it is the story that is incredible. I had forgotten the powerful lesson this little book contains. Even the most miserable of us are not beyond the possibility of a better life. When Roberts brought this in from the lawn I nearly threw it into the fireplace, but something made me not only hold on to it but read it as well. The results you can see for yourself." She smiled and put her arms around Thomas and whispered, "Thank you for trespassing, dear boy."

Mr. McPherson broke the silence that followed by calling for a toast.

"Wait a moment, please. I have one more person to attend to. Which one of you lovely young ladies is Penny?"

Penny stepped forward. "I am, Miss Groves."

"Well, well. I can't say that I blame Thomas for risking his life and my limbs for you. Roberts, would you please get what we left in the car?"

Roberts went to the car and returned with a tall crystal vase filled with peacock tail feathers.

"Oh, Miss Groves," Penny said as she accepted the gift. "I don't know what to say."

Miss Groves saw tears rising in the girl's eyes and to save her from embarrassment pointed to Mr. McPherson and said, "Now, you were about to propose a toast I believe."

Mr. McPherson raised his glass and said in a loud voice, "To Mr. Charles Dickens, a man who wrote stories that have healed hearts, mended souls, and changed lives for over a hundred and fifty years. God bless him and all such writers!"

"Hear, hear," cried Mr Cody and Mr. Gilson who just that moment arrived with more Champagne and sherry and a furiously flaming Christmas pudding! Mae rushed to the door to help Mr. Gilson escape a premature cremation! "I swear! You two should not be allowed to play with matches!" she said. The men looked sheepish and promised they would forgo their dramatic entrance next year. No one within hearing believed them!

Glasses were raised and, in this abundance of joy, Thomas and Penny made their escape to the front yard where they stood close together gazing through tree limbs at the stars. The air was crisp and perfumed with wood smoke.

"It has been a grand day," Penny said.

"Certainly has."

"I love my bookmark."

"I'm glad."

Penny leaned closer and Thomas thought he would lose his balance. "There's just one more thing to add to this day that would make it perfect, but we haven't any mistletoe."

Thomas swallowed hard and hoped his voice would not crack when he said, "There's a bunch in this tree. Do you want me to climb up and get some?"

"Thomas Hardy Godwin! That's not even funny! You stay right where you are! Besides, I don't think the tradition says anything about how close the mistletoe must be to the top of your head. That bunch way up there could serve the purpose just fine. Don't you agree?"

Without saying a word, Thomas showed Penny that, yes indeed, he did agree.

ABOUT THE AUTHOR

Here's how these stories came to be:

I was seated comfortably in my favorite chair one Saturday in October 1998, looking forward to an afternoon of watching college football, when my wife, Candace, came into the den with a section of our neighborhood newspaper folded to a page that read:

"EVER DREAM OF WRITING THE GREAT AMERICAN NOVEL? HOW ABOUT THE GREAT AMERICAN CHRISTMAS STORY?"

It was a contest. The paper wanted an original, fictional, Christmas story to publish in their holiday supplement. Contestants were advised when and where to submit their entry and what prize the winner could expect.

Candace dropped the paper in my lap and said one word before leaving the room: "Enter."

Well, I won that year, and the year after that, and the year after that. In 2001, the paper's editor told me that she and her staff and subscribers had grown to expect a "Thomas story" each year so the contest was ended and for the next seven years I appeared in mid-November at the paper's offices with another one.

It was inevitable that Thomas would grow up and move on. I wrote the last story in this collection over ten years ago; I left Thomas with Penny, and Mae with Mr. Gilson and I thought that would be the last time they would enter my imagination. I was wrong. Stay tuned.

Charles Robert Baker

October 2019

Made in the USA
San Bernardino, CA
12 December 2019